I0517067

The Power Of Love: 2 Short Stories

by Nikida Bellezza

The Power Of Love 2 Short Stories by Nikida Bellezza

The Power Of Love 2 Short Stories by Nikida Bellezza

I am eternally grateful to be blessed with the art of story telling. It's the only thing I can do all day, and all night and still feel refreshed when I am done. Writing is my escape from everything. I hope that while reading my creation, you're able to join me in this fascinating land of make believe, even if only for a little while.

Thank you for reading,

-Nikida

JUST HOLD ME DOWN

a Nikida Bellezza short

CHAPTER 1

"Damn that shit was good." I said as I fell backwards onto the bed.

"No muhfuckin bullshit. Damn girl, you got full control over that snatch!" Devon agreed as he sat up and reached inside his nightstand.

"Fuck yeah!" I boasted with a chuckle.

"Yeah, you hittin' this jay wit me?" He asked as he started rolling.

"Nah, I got to go pick up my son from daycare." I replied swinging my legs around to get out of the bed. I reached down for my clothes so that I could start getting dressed. I knew that I was pushing it time wise, but that last nut had me bawling like a baby it felt so damn good. Besides I knew that if it really came down to me being late, they'd just call De'Sean, my baby father to come get him. At least that was what the horny bitch in me reasoned.

"Aright, you be easy and all that otha' good shit!" He mumbled while licking the blunt closed.

"Likewise." I replied before leaving out and heading down to my car.

After getting into my car, I noticed the message alert light flashing on my cell, so I grabbed it to see that I had four missed calls from Sean.

Shaking my head, not even in the mood for this argument, I hit send, to call him back. He always gave me grief when he had to call me more than once. One thing I can say about him though, even for all the dirt I knew that he was doing in the streets, when I hit him, he'd always answer me on the first call, or hit me back right after. I never had to search for him or blow up his phone.

"Yeah man, where you been jo?" He asked sounding irritated as he answered the phone.

"Out! why, what's up?" I barked back.

"Man, I been tryn' catch you before you went over to Vinny's school. Ms. Melanie said he got in a fight and we needed to come get him ASAP." Sean said.

"So you got him?" I asked as I started up my car.

"yeah, I got him. Fuck wrong wit you?" He asked.

"Nigga, you give me all that attitude as soon as I get on the phone, then ask what's wrong with *me*?" I shot back.

"Whateva' jo, you on your way home or what?" He asked.

"I might be." I replied messing with him.

"Yeah, aright." He said sucking his teeth.

"Bye." I said before I ended the call.

De'Sean and I had been together since our senior year of high school. He went to Woodson in DC and I graduated from Suitland in Maryland. We met at a mutual friends cookout, and have been together every since. I loved the man more than I could love anybody, and I knew he felt the same about me. But when I found out he was cheating on me, instead of bringing it to his attention, I felt two could play that game. I knew that he could tell something was messed up on my end, but he couldn't bring it up because he was messing up on his end as well. So we both played the nut roll and lived out our lives as though everything was everything.

When I got home I dropped my purse on the couch and walked back to Vinny's room. He was laying on his bed playing his game.

"Mommy!" He exclaimed excitedly when he noticed me.

"Hey baby, what's going on? What happened in school?" I asked as I sat on his bed and gave him a hug.

"Jonny hit me with a toy, so I punched him in the mouth like daddy told me to. But he was bleeding so I got in trouble." Vinny explained.

"That's what the fuck he get too!" Sean declared as he walked into the room. Vinny and I both looked over at him.

"Bet he leave you alone now!" He added with a chuckle.

"But if I was right, why I get in trouble?" Vinny asked.

"Because your teacher some shit." Sean replied casually.

"*SEAN!*" I yelled.

"*What*, its true!" Sean retorted.

"Baby, you got in trouble because your teacher has to make sure that people are safe in her classroom, and even though you didn't hit first, you hit the hardest..."

"Like you was supposed to." Sean said interrupting me.

"*SO...* because you hit the hardest, it made the other kid unsafe. The teacher had to do what she thought was best." I explained with ease.

"But that's not *fair!*" Vinny cried out.

"At *all!*" Sean said instigating. I shot Sean a look before turning my attention back towards Vinny.

"Baby, just because your teacher thought it was right, doesn't mean it's going to be fair. Not everybody thinks the same, so fair means different things to different people." I said just as Vinny started laughing. That's when I noticed Sean's shadow against the wall making boxing movements. When I turned around to look at him he stopped and looked at me as if to be asking '*What?'*

"What's up?" Sean asked innocently.

7

"I can't with you." I said as I stood to leave the room.

"But where you goin' though?" He asked as I walked passed him.

"To make dinner." I replied throwing a dismissive hand at him as I headed down the hall.

After we ate, Sean put Vinny in the tub while I washed dishes. Then we tucked him in and read him a bedtime story which put him to sleep.

"I'm 'bout to go take a shower." I said once we were in the hall outside of Vinny's room.

"I'll bet." Sean said as he headed back to our bedroom.

"Fuck that's supposed to mean?" I asked rocking my head with my hands on my hips. He looked back at me and shook his head with a shoulder shrug.

"Shit." He replied then he continued into the bedroom.

"Yeah, whatever." I said with a chuckle to myself.

I took a nice long hot shower, slowly washing Devon's touch, licks and kisses off my body. While he ain't have shit on Sean, he was no slouch when it came to sex. He did everything I wanted and liked and he allowed me to take full control. Sean didn't mind me taking control, but he was an Alpha male, so relinquishing control was a little harder for him. It wasn't so much that he was controlling, he just always wanted to be sure that I was good.

After my shower I put on lotion, and brushed my teeth.

When I got back into the room I saw Sean laying across the bed watching TV.

Using the towel I had wrapped around myself, I dried off then I put on my pajamas.

"Why you never sleep naked no more?" He asked never taking his eyes off the TV.

"Because we have a son now, and he can come in here any time of night." I said with an attitude.

"Shit, I'm just askin' slim, you ain't gotta gimme all that." He said.

"Nah you just seem to have a lot of smart ass shit to say. I'm just waiting for you to get whatever it is you *really* got to say off your chest." I replied as I walked over to the bed.

"Gotdamn, I can't even ask a muthafuckin question in this bitch." He said, more to himself.

"Nigga what?" I asked hearing the word bitch although knowing he'd never call me one, I decided to get in my feelings anyway.

He turned around and looked at me like I was crazy.

"Fuck wrong witchu?" He asked.

"I'm sayin', I know I heard the word bitch. I'm just tryin' figure out the context." I said.

"First of all slim, don't do that. You know I ain't call you no bitch. I never have, why would I start now? Second, you comin' at me real strong right now. If you got somethin' to say, you need to just say that shit, or keep all that attitude to yourself." He said seriously.

"Whateva, good night!" I said as I lay down and pulled the covers up.

That night as I slept, my mind began to recall events that happened to me fifteen years before when I was kidnapped by my neighbor Mr. McGill. He held me hostage for three days before I was able to escape. I was fourteen years old when he told me he had some of my parents mail in his home and asked me to come get it.

I followed him inside where he closed and locked the door behind me. He dragged me to a room in the basement where he took my virginity. For three days he made me watch porn and he forced me to do the things we saw in the video with him. On the third night while he was away I busted out of his house and ran to tell my parents. My dad grabbed his gun, a few friends and searched for months for him, but he was never found.

9

I woke up from the dream already sobbing and crying as though I had been doing this in my sleep.

"Mmmh, Lisha." I heard Sean say as he turned over. But I didn't reply.

I felt him put his arms around me and pull me close.

"You dreamed about him again?" He asked familiar with my dreams. I nodded my head as I turned over and lay my head on his chest.

"I swear to god, if I ever find that nigga I will murder his ass." Sean said as he held me.

"Nobody can find him, he's still out there." I sobbed.

"Trust me, if cuz breathin', he can be found, especially if he in this city." Sean said.

"I don't want to talk about it anymore." I said as I moved as close to him as I could get.

"Aright baby, we won't, just go 'head and try to get some sleep. I got you, you good, aright." He said.

"I can't sleep, I don't want to see his face." I cried.

"Then we can just stay up. Whateva you want." Sean assured me.

"But you have to go to work in a few, tomorrow is Thursday." I said.

"Lisha, let me worry about that, aright. I'm good, this is more important to me right now." He said.

"I love you Sean." I said.

"I love you too baby girl" He replied as he gently stroked my head.

We stayed up for another hour until I was able to fall asleep, which happened to be an hour and a half before he had to get up for work.

Although I was asleep, I felt him kiss my cheek before he left out.

When my alarm went off three hours later, I got up and went to use the bathroom. I washed my face, brushed my teeth and went back to my room to get dressed for work.

"Morning Mommy!" Vinny said as he walked into my room just as I fastened the strap on my heel.

"Morning favorite!" I said as I walked over to him and scooped him into my arms.

"What's for breakfast?" He asked.

"Cereal." I answered while carrying him into the kitchen. I sat him at the table and proceeded to make his breakfast. Afterward I dressed him and we headed out.

This morning I took him to my parents' house which was just a few minutes away, because of his little suspension from daycare.

When I pulled up to the house I parked and Vinny and I raced to the door.

"I beat you mommy! I run fast!" Vinny boasted as I pretended to be out of breath.

"Yes, I gotta get more energy to keep up with you!" I said

"Yeah, and daddy too!" He cheered as I used my to key to open the door.

"Morning!" I called aloud as I walked inside my parents' home.

"Morning, I'm in my room!" My mother said.

Vinny and I walked back to her room and found her ironing my dad's shirt.

"Hey ma, where's daddy?" I asked kissing her cheek.

"In the shower, hey Vin Vin! How's my grand-baby?" My mother asked as she swooped him up in her arms.

"Good! I got 'spended from day care." He said.

"You got suspended, and yes I heard!" My mother said as she sat him on her bed.

"Aright ma, I gotta go to work. Sean will be by later to pick him up." I said.

"Okay baby, have a good day now." She said as she and Vinny walked me to the door.

"See you later favorite!" I said as I leaned down towards him.

"By mommy." He said before giving me a kiss on the cheek.

When I got to work I was a little early so I walked into the break room to get myself a cup of coffee.

"Morning Alisha," I heard my coworker Charles call from the table.

"What's up Chuck?" I asked as I poured my coffee.

"So you know they up'd our quota's right. Now they want us to average fifty calls an hour." He said as he grabbed a bagel.

"That ain't nothin', I do that anyway." I replied adding cream.

"Well go shawty, its ya birthday!" He replied sarcastically.

"Whose birthday?" Paula, another coworker asked as she walked into the break room.

"Nobody's he just being funny, or trying to be. So I heard they upped the quota." I said before sipping my coffee.

"yeah girl, fifty calls an hour. I can barely get through twenty calls. I fuckin hate this damn job!" She said sounding irritated.

"Well reverse time and take yo ass to college instead then." Charles sassed.

"Chuck, shut yo ass up!" Paula exclaimed throwing a piece of her muffin at him.

"Y'all crazy, I'm about to go clock in." I chuckled as i left the break room.

After work I headed to the grocery store to pick up a few things before going home.

When I got in the house I saw Sean helping Vinny with some work his teacher sent home with him yesterday.

"What's up?" Sean asked as I walked through the door.

"Shit, what's good?" I asked back heading towards the kitchen.

"You got more bags?" He called behind me.

"Nah, just this." I said as I started taking the food out.

"Mommy, I finished my work, can I go to the playground?" Vinny asked running into the kitchen behind me. I turned around and leaned against the counter.

"You wait til I get home for this?" I asked aloud so that Sean would know that I was talking to him.

"What you *mean*?" He asked from the living room.

"He just asked me could he go outside." I said folding my arms.

"Aright, *can* he?" Sean asked.

I walked back into the living room to see Sean playing his game system.

"Hold up, how you playin' that already when you was just helpin' him with his work?" I asked.

"It was already hooked up. Damn, what, you had a bad day?" He asked glancing over at me for a half a second.

"Nah, but I ain't been home for four hours yet *either*!" I said with my hands on my hips.

"Aright man damn. Vin go put on your play shoes and lets go." Sean said still playing his game.

"Yaaay!" Vinny said as he ran back to his room.

"*Thank* you!" I said before leaving the living room.

"I mean, can dinner at least be ready when we come back tho?" He yelled behind me.

"I ain't makin' no promises." I said as I went into the bathroom to start my bath.

13

I grabbed my bubble bath off the shelf and added it to the water. Then I went into the bedroom to get my robe.

Once the water and bubbles were high enough I turned the water off, took off my clothes and stepped inside. The hot water was so soothing it almost brought on an orgasm.

I grabbed my headphones and put them in my ear as I searched through the play-lists in my phone.

"Oh, that's why you tryn' get rid of us, you in one of them moods." Sean said as he walked in the bathroom.

"Privacy please!" I exclaimed.

"Yeah whateva'. If you goin' have them headphones on, don't have 'em loud, you 'bout to be in here alone. You need to be able to hear." Sean said before leaving the bathroom.

"I'm good!" I said aloud.

"You heard me!" He yelled back before I heard the door close.

A few minutes later my phone buzzed through my music. Irritated thinking that It was Sean, I snatched up my phone and hit the button to turn on the light. But to my surprise it was Devon asking for another go, and of course I obliged his request, agreeing to meet up with him later in the week.

I replied "Of course." Then I sat my phone back down and slid into the warm bubbles to continue my relaxation.

CHAPTER 2

The following weekend Sean and I decided to go shopping out Arundel Mills Mall, just to get out of the area and get some things we needed a wanted.

The mall was huge and it was much different from anything we had in the city, even in the surrounding areas. We liked it because it was closer than Potomac mills and it was rare that we would run into anybody that we knew. Even Sean, who seemed to know everybody, every damn where.

"Mommy, can you get me a new bike?" Vinny asked while we walked by a toy store with a display of bikes in the window.

"Maybe next time baby." I replied trying to get passed the store as quickly as possible.

"What's wrong wit the bike you got now, lil homie?" Sean asked him.

"It's got training wheels, like I'm a baby, but I'm a big boy!" He said throwing his arms in the air.

"Awww that ain't nothin'. I'll just take 'em off when we get home, and I'll show you how to ride, cool?" Sean asked.

"Cool." Vinny replied.

"Aye, I'm bout to go to this shoe store real quick, where you goin' be?" Sean asked me.

"I'm trying to find a clothing store." I said

"Bet, do that and I'll meet you in the food court in like fi'teen minutes, aright." He said.

"When have you ever known me to only be in a store for fifteen minutes, mind you, I haven't even found one yet." I said with my hands on my hips.

"We goin' be in this joint all day, ain't we?" He asked with a sigh.

15

"I thought that was the plan, *family day*, or have you found something else more important to do?" I asked giving up straight attitude.

"Slim, don't you eva' get tired of arguing? I mean for real?" He asked.

"I mean, don't *you*?" I asked back.

He shook his head as he walked over to me and slipped an arm around my waist. Then he snatched me up against his body and kissed me.

"I'll be in the shoe store, I'll find you." He said after he pulled away.

"Oh, okay." I said trying to regain myself.

"You comin' wit me, or you stayin' wit mommy?" He asked Vinny.

"Can I get a toy?" He asked.

"This nigga, my own son tryn' bargain wit me. Yeah man, you can get a toy, let's bounce." Sean said with a chuckle.

"Aright, see y'all in a bit." I said as Vinny walked over to his dad.

"You got enough on you?" Sean asked me.

"Yeah, I'm straight." I replied.

"Cool, be safe, take your phone off silent." He said.

"i-i captain." I replied.

"At ease." He said before he and Vinny walked away.

I walked around the mall until I found a store that I felt suited me.

I was in there for all of thirty minutes when Sean called me.

"Yeah?" I asked answering the phone.

"Where you at shawty?" He asked.

"Wet Seal." I replied searching through some shirts.

"You almost done?" He asked.

"Why, whats wrong?" I asked annoyed

"Man, I just asked you a question, slim. We hungry." Sean said.

"Aright, let me just go pay for what I got and I'll meet yall in the food court." I replied.

"Aright, mah'fact, what you want, so we can already be in one of these long ass lines." He said.

"It don't matter, whatever yall get is cool." I replied happy to have few more minutes to shop.

"Bet, aright." He said then we hung up the phone.

Once I made my purchase I left the store and walked to the food court.

When I got there, all I saw were tons of lines snaking away from the lil strip of restaurants. I searched around for Sean and Vinny, but I couldn't see them.

During one of my scans my eyes did catch something that stopped my heart. It was Mr. McGill, he seemed to be headed straight for me, but he wasn't looking at me, at least not at first.

The shock of seeing him and being alone again froze me and seemed to slow down my mental as I felt myself drop everything in my hand.

With my heart pounding heavy, and my breath getting short, I was now in full panic mode. I forced my eyes to move around the room to find Sean. Finally I saw him running over to me, but he seemed to be moving in slow motion with everything else, even as he called my name.

Mr. McGill looked at me and smiled, licking his lips. I noticed him moving his head to look around me, I suppose to see if I were alone. Then smiled harder as his motioned himself towards me.

"Sean, Sean..." Was all that I could say as I felt my breath getting shorter.

"Lisha, what, what happened, what is it?" Sean asked once he approached me. That's when I saw Mr. McGill take off running.

My eyes fearfully followed him running through the mall. Sean followed my eyes to see what I was looking at. Finally he noticed a person who seemed to be running for their lives.

"That's *him*?" He yelled.

I nodded my head as I watched Mr. McGill knock people over in his pursuit to get away. He actually moved quite fast for an older man.

"Lisha, take Vinny, and go home. NOW... GO!" Sean said before he took off after Mr McGill.

"Sean!" I screamed after him.

"GO, HOME!" He hollered back.

"Mommy, what's wrong? Where's daddy going?" Vinny exclaimed.

"It's okay baby." I said as my son's voice knocked me out of my trance.

"Here mommy, you dropped this." Vinny said as he handed me my bags.

"Thank you baby, come on, let's go." I said as I took his little hand.

We walked out to the truck where I loaded the bags and helped him into his car seat. Then I got in and started it up.

"What the fuck?" I said to myself as I shook my head and rested it against the steering wheel.

"You okay mommy?" Vinny asked.

"Yes baby, I'm good, come on lets go." I said as I started up Sean's truck.

"What about daddy?" Vinny asked

"He's gonna come home later baby. He had something he needed to do." I said wondering myself how he'd get all the way back to DC from Anne Arundel County.

The two of us rode back in silence. Vinny eventually fell asleep along the way.

But my mind was going a hundred miles a minute, racing over thoughts of *'What if I were there alone',* and *'What if Sean catches Mr. McGill',* I also found myself battling attempts to suppress the memories of my kidnapping experience from resurfacing.

I don't even know how, but I made it back to DC in one piece.

I dropped Vinny off with my parents for the night. I told them that Sean and I needed a night alone. Being a hopeless romantic, my mom took my lie and ate it up.

Finally, when I got home, I lay next to my phone and once again I leased my thoughts to replay the events of the day.

Why was Mr. McGill smiling and coming towards me, what did he want? Why did I freeze up like that? I felt like I was that same lil girl in a helpless situation. I was just as terrified today as I was when it all happened. I had so many questions yet no answers.

Several hours later I heard the door to the apartment open and close. I jumped up out of bed and ran out to the living room where Sean was taking off his shirts.

"Hey." I said softly, trying to feel him out.

"What's up?" He asked as he tucked his shirt up under his arm, almost as though he was trying to hide it from me.

"Nothin" I shrugged.

"How you feel, are you okay, after seeing that bitchass nigga?" He asked with a concerned frown.

19

"I don't know. It was like I was fourteen all over again." I said shaking my head as the tears started to fall.

Sean walked over to me and put his arms around me.

"Let me go take a shower real quick. I'll meet you in the room okay." He said after he let me go.

"Okay." I replied still needing to be in his arms.

I walked back to the bedroom and sat on the bed against the headboard biting my nails waiting for my protector to return to me.

Fifteen minutes later Sean came out of the bathroom in a towel.

I watched him dry off, then he put on his boxers, some basketball shorts and a t-shirt.

Then he walked over, and lie across the bed and wrapped his arms around my thighs and used my stomach as his pillow.

"Vinny at your mom's?" He asked.

"Yeah, I told her we just needed some time." I replied.

"Cool." He said sounding exhausted.

"Sean, what happened at the mall, and how did you get home? I asked.

"Shit, and I know people" He replied nonchalantly.

"I can't *know*?" I asked.

"Don't I tell you everything you need to know?" He asked looking up at me.

"yeah." I replied.

"And what do I say about everything else?" He asked.

"Trust you." I answered, reciting the speech he always gives me.

"Right, that's what I need from you right now. I don't feel like talkin', I don't feel like answering or askin' questions. I just want to make sure you good, and fall asleep. That's all I got left for today." He said before yawning.

"Okay." I said as I reached over and turned off the lamp. He sat up for me to slide under him, then he wrapped his arms around me and eventually we fell asleep.

The next day I woke up to the smell of bacon cooking. I stood up to stretch before heading into the Kitchen where Sean was at the stove cooking breakfast.

"Morning." I said going into refrigerator to grab the orange juice.

"What's up, I hope you hungry, I just made this big ass breakfast." He said glancing back at me.

"Yeah, I'm starving." I replied as I grabbed a glass from the cabinet.

"Beeet!" He sang flipping the bacon.

"So what you doin' today?" I inquired, wondering what the big breakfast was all about.

"Chillin' wit you." He answered casually.

"It's Sunday, you not playin' ball?" I asked sitting at the table.

"If I was playin' ball, I'd already be out there." He said.

"Whatever." I responded before sipping my juice.

"I can't win with you shawty, a nigga just can't win!" He said with a chuckle as he turned up his music. He had been listening to some gogo. I smiled as I stood up to leave.

I went to take a shower, and to put on some house clothes.

After breakfast we lay across the couch and watched a couple movies. Then we played a few board games and got bored, so he decided to teach me how to play his game system.

We spent the entire day together, no phones, no leaving the house, nothing, we even took a nap together.

Later that night we lay in bed and held hands as we listened to the rain fall.

"This was the best day that we've had in a long time." I said.

"No doubt." He replied.

"I wish we'd have more like this." I said.

"We will." He assured.

"I hope so." I added as I put my arms around him.

"Lisha, it's time we made some changes in our lives." He said.

"What you mean?" I asked confused.

"Let's just keep it one hunid, I know about cuz, just like you know about my side chicks." He said.

"What are you talkin' about?" I asked playing dumb.

"Come on slim, don't do that, I just said we keepin' it one hunid. I know you know about them, just like I know about cuz. We both wrong, we both fucked up, but now it it's time to cut that shit off. It's time for us to do us, one hunid percent." He said.

"Okay." I replied knowing that he knew what he was talking about.

"If cuz don't understand that it's a done deal, let me know, so I can help him with his comprehension." Sean said.

"And if them bitches don't know..." I started but he cut me off.

"I got them, trust me, don't nobody challenge me but you." He said.

"So why the change anyway? I asked after a few moments of silence

"Here you go with that." he said as he shook his head.

"No I'm serious, why now?" I asked concerned as he seemed to really have something on his mind.

"Because, you're going to be my wife, and I need all of you." He said.

"And I'll have all of you?" I asked.

"No doubt." He said.

"Sean, I can tell that you're worried about something. What is it?" I asked.

He turned over and lay his head on my chest as he stretched his arm across my stomach.

"Rub my head baby girl" He said which meant he was done talking. I complied as my mind began to wonder about what was troubling him. Sean wasn't big on allowing others to worry for or about him. The only thing he ever required of me to do in the way of helping him during difficult times, was to be quiet and lay with him. I hated not knowing what was going on, but he felt better when I didn't, and instead trusted in him enough to know that he would make whatever it was alright.

I loved him, and even though I gave him grief, when it came down to it, there was nothing I wouldn't do for him, and he felt the same. Little did I know, the proof in that would come much sooner than later.

CHAPTER 3

That Tuesday, which was two days later was a holiday so Sean didn't have to work, but my office was open and I had to go in.

I had to force myself awake from what was probably the most comfortable sleep I had in a while. I dragged myself into the shower, then I dressed and styled my hair.

Once I was done, I went into the living room where Sean was playing his game.

"Aright, I'm bout to roll out." I said as I stepped into my heels.

"Aright baby, call your mom and tell her I'll be there to scoop Vinny in about an hour, I just need to put my clothes on." He said.

"Okay." I replied just as we heard three loud thumps against the door.

"What the fuck?" Sean said as he dropped his controller on the table and moved me out of the way.

"Who is it?" He asked.

"It's the Police, we're here for a De'Sean Taylor." Came a voice from the other side of the door.

"Sean!" I said as I touched his arm. He walked over to the door and opened it.

"DeSean Taylor?" The big burly cop who was accompanied by two others asked.

"Yeah." Sean replied as if he were asking them "What's up?"

"You are under arrest for the murder of Randolph McGill. You're going to have to come with us." The cop said

"Oh my gawd!" I cried

"Aright, let me just hug her goodbye." Sean said respectfully.

24

"One minute son." The cop said. Sean nodded his head before turning around to come to me.

"Sean, what's going on?" I asked. He leaned in and put his arms around me.

"Go in the closet, pull up the carpet in the corner, take out the box, and punch in your birthday. There's a card at the bottom, call the number on the card and ask him how much. When he tell you, take that out of the box and put the box back. I'ma call you when they let me make a call. I love you, do as I say." He said then he kissed my lips.

"Sean, whats going on?" I asked.

"Trust me." He said then he walked over to the cops who read him his rights as they cuffed him, then they took him away.

I felt scared and helpless. There was nothing that I could do to stop them from taking the love of my life away.

Sean was my backbone, my support, the only reason I knew that I was okay, was because he made me know that I was.

I walked over to the window just in time to see them ease his head down before putting him into the backseat. Once he was secured inside the car they closed the door.

He looked up at our window, when he saw me, he mouthed the words 'I love you.' Then he smiled and winked.

"I love you too." I said back just as they were pulling out. I watched them drive him away, taking my total sense of security with him. I never thought I'd have to survive without Sean, and now, I was given no choice.

"Oh Sean." I said as the tears started blurring my vision. I could barely wrap my mind around all that had just happened, and whats more, was it true?

Was Sean a murderer? Did he actually kill Mr. McGill? I knew that he said he would, but I never actually believed that he was about that life.

I thought back to when we kicked around war stories in high school and how he used to tell me he'd beat niggas unconscious and eventually it got around that he wasn't that nigga to fuck with. But even still, he never mentioned that anyone died after taking a beating from him.

Sean was very strong, I discovered that when I broke my toe by kicking a stone at the park, and he had to carry me two blocks to our car. He didn't complain, he just kept saying *'I got you baby.'*

I shook my head as I took out my cell to call my job. I needed to inform them that I wouldn't be in today due to a family emergency.

Once I squared things away with them, I walked back to the bedroom where I had a seat on the bed. I had so much thinking to do. First of all, what do I tell Vinny about why his daddy isn't here.

What if Sean is found guilty and is sentenced to life or something. Every since they closed Lorton, they've been sending DC inmates to different parts of the country, I wouldn't even at least be near him.

These painful thoughts welcomed a fresh crop of tears that I cried into my hands.

Eventually I lay back on the bed and cried myself to sleep.

I woke up a couple hours later to the sound of my phone ringing. Thinking that it could be Sean I jumped to my feet and ran over to answer it.

"Hello?" I shouted into the phone.

"Collect call from District Of Columbia Correctional Facility, do you accept the chargers?" I heard an operator's voice ask.

"Yes." I replied

"Please hold ma'am." The operator said.

"What's up baby girl, how you holdin' up?" Sean's voice asked.

"I'm not, not without you." I said.

"Let me tell you somethin', with or without me, you'd be good." He said.

"Don't say that. I don't want to be without you." I whined.

"I know, and I don't want to be without you either. You and Vinny are the whole reason I exist." He said.

"We feel the same way baby." I said as tears came to my eyes.

"Bet that. So I see you ain't do what I asked you to do." He said with a chuckle. It took me all of ten seconds to realize what he was talking about.

"No, not yet, I forgot. But how you know that anyway?" I said. He sighed into the phone.

"Because you would've had something to say. But Look baby, I don't ask you to do much, so when I do ask you to do something, you know it's important." He stated calmly.

"I know baby, I just had so much on my mind, I forgot." I pleaded, not wanting him to feel that he couldn't count on me when he needed me the most.

"I know you do, and I'm sorry for even being the cause of all that. But this is like up there on the important scale. I need you to handle that for me asap, then come see me tomorrow, okay?" He said.

"Okay." I replied.

"Aright, you know where I'm at right, over there by DC General." He said.

"Yeah, I know." I answered.

"Bet, let me get off this phone before they disconnect this call. I love you baby girl" He said.

"I love you too." I said as I started to cry again.

"Be strong for me shawty. I need you to save them tears for something happy, daddy good, believe me." He said.

"Qkay." I said.

"See you tomorrow." He said.

"okay, bye." I replied before ending the call.

I looked over at the closet for a few seconds, then I stood up and walked over.

I moved shoes and boxes out of the way in order to get to the carpet as he instructed.

Then I pulled up the carpet and found the box that he was talking about.

Seconds after I punched in my birthday for the code, the box flipped open to reveal bundles and bundles and bundles of money. Hundreds, fifties, and twenties all neatly folded and secured by rubber bands and clips.

"What the FUCK?!" I exclaimed shocked to shit.

The box was wide and deep and there was money to the depths of it.

My eyes slowly roamed the contents of the box. Never had I ever seen so much money in my life. My palms began to itch as though they just couldn't wait to touch it. As the initial shock wore off, I began to remember my purpose and proceeded to do as I was told.

I slipped my hand all the way down until I was elbows deep, which brought me to the bottom. There I felt around until I felt paper that didn't feel like money. I gripped it and pulled it out to see that it was a small square card, shaped like a business card but it only had a phone number on it. I went to grab my cell off the bed and dialed the number.

"Yep." I heard a man with a scratchy voice say.

"Uh, how much?" I asked nearly forgetting my line.

"Seventy Kay." He said then he hung up the phone.

"Seventy kay, is that seventy thousand or what?" I asked myself as I looked down at all the money.

Just to be safe I did count out Seventy-Thousand dollars before closing the case and replacing it. I covered the area then I went into the kitchen to put the money into an envelope and stuffed it under the mattress.

Suddenly I was aware of everything, every sound in the house, every car that drove by, every voice I heard in the distance. Everyone was coming to get me for this money. Everyone was plotting on how to get rid of me to get their hands on it. My mind led me into a place that left me terrified. A few minutes later the house phone rang again, this time I nearly jumped out of my skin.

"Hello?" I asked answering the phone.

"What you doin home? I thought I'd be cussing Sean out about not coming to get Vinny this morning, I had to take him with me to my pottery class!" My mother exclaimed.

"Ma, Sean was arrested this morning, I don't know the details, but I'm sorry that I forgot to call you. I've just been going crazy over here." I said.

"Lord have mercy, are you okay?" She asked concerned.

"No, he is my life ma, I don't know what to do. I go see him tomorrow, maybe then he'll be able to tell me something." I said.

"okay, well, don't worry, I'll keep Vinny until yall figure all this out." She said.

"Thanks ma." I replied. We talked for about an hour then I ended the call.

I woke up the next morning, called my job and told them I needed to use emergency leave, and that I'd need to be out for the entire week. I hated that I had to disclose the details, but I was happy that my job was understanding. After I got off the phone with them, I hopped into the shower, dressed and headed for the jail.

When I got there I parked and damn near ran into the building. Once inside, I gave my name, was frisked and some more, then they had me sit in a waiting area.

The wait was the hardest part. It seemed to last for ever. As boredom began to strike, I found myself looking around at the people who were also there to see loved ones. I noticed sets of women with children running all around, screaming and playing. Older women looking so tired and worn, you could tell that they were fed up and were just plain ready to give up. And many young guys who all seemed to know each other although they discussed being there to see different people.

Just based off the waiting area that day, DC jail seemed more like a rec center from the outside looking in, everybody met their homies up there to chill.

"Daniels, did you see who was being checked in?" Asked one of two cops standing at the window.

"No, who?" The one named Daniels replied.

"That goddamn Jew!" The first cop said.

"*Goldberg*?" Daniels asked looking up from his paperwork.

"Fuckin' right! I wonder which one of these cock suckers in here got him to come up here to see them?!" The first cop said asked visibly upset.

"Who can afford him is the better question." Daniels asked.

"Awe these monkey's got drug money. A few thousand ain't nothin to them! The shit sickens me I tell ya. I work hard every day of my life and have less to show for it than a goddamn inmate!" The first cop said.

"Calm down there. let's first find out who he's here to see, then we'll go from there. If this asshole is gonna get off scott free, we can at least delay him." Daniels said with a pat to the first cops back.

"Now you're talkin buddy!" The first cop said as they both started laughing.

"Taylor, DeSean, visitor come on back!" I heard a female voice call out.

I stood up and walked back through the doors.

Once inside the visiting room I looked around for Sean. He was sitting at a table already looking over at me smiling. I couldn't help but return the smile as I happily walked over to him.

"Hey baby girl, damn it's good to see you, even though it ain't been but a day." He said standing to hug me.

"Toughest night I ever had." I replied as I put my arms around him.

"I know baby, how'd you sleep?" He asked once we let go.

"Off and on." I answered with a shrug. We both took a seat at the table.

"So how's Vinny?" He asked.

"He's okay, my mother said she'd keep him until we figured all of this out." I replied.

"Bet, so thank you for handlin' that lil business I asked you to handle for me too." He said as he took my hands.

"How'd you know I did it?" I asked surprised.

"Because he's coming to see me today, after you leave." He replied.

31

"Wait, is his name Goldberg?" I asked wondering if Sean could be the mystery person Goldberg was coming to see. Sean sat back with a curious look on his face.

"How you know that name?" He asked.

"Because some cops were in the waiting area trying to figure out who he was here to see. They said something about delaying something." I said trying to recall the story.

"Oh really. Hmmm." Sean said as he sat forward again and rubbed his chin.

"Baby, what's going on?" I asked. He looked over at me and smiled.

"Just a very concentrated game of chess. Don't worry about nothin, I got this. But look baby, i'ma need you to do one more thing for me. Add another dub to that total, then put all of it in one of them big brown envelopes and mail it to an address that you're about to get on your way out of here." He said.

"What? Why would I get an address on the way out of here?" I asked confused.

"Lish, this ain't the time to be asking questions baby. This one of them things where I'm tellin' you what you need to know, and I need you to trust me on the rest." He said.

"okay baby, whatever you want." I replied with a sigh.

"The code on the box is different now, it's my birthday this time, okay." He said.

"okay." I replied looking down.

"I promise you baby, all this will be over soon." He said as he reached for my hands. I looked up at him and nodded my head.

"I love you Sean." I said.

"I love you more." He replied.

We talked for another five minutes before they called for me to leave. I hugged and kissed him for as long as I could before they screamed at me to leave.

On the way out I kept turning around to look at Sean who was leaning back against the wall looking at me. I didn't notice the guy coming into the door and we collided causing some papers to fall from his hand.

"Oh, my bad." I said as I tried to help him gather his things.

"No worries young lady, here, I believe you dropped this." He said handing me a card.

I looked down at it to see a handwritten address across the front. I looked up at the man who smiled and walked away before I could say anything else. I knew that this was Sean's doing so I didn't look back, I just stuffed the card into my purse and headed out.

After leaving the jail I stopped off at the store to grab some brown envelopes, the kind with the bubble wrap inside, then I went straight home.

As I walked into the door I felt my phone vibrating in my purse. Wishing that it was Sean calling to tell me that it was all a mistake, I threw everything on the couch. I rummaged through my purse and snatched up my phone to see that it was Devon.

"Damn nigga, ain't I the one that's suppose to call you?!" I exclaimed just before answering my phone.

"What's up?" I asked annoyed.

"That pussy, what's good?" He asked.

"Look Devon, we can't get down like that no more, me and my man tryn' make it work, so all that's over." I replied.

"Damn shawty, its like that though? I can't get no severance pussy though?" He asked.

"Oh so what, I was the only one you was fuckin?" I asked calling him weak.

"Fuck outta here, I get pussy like the air, your shit just real good though, know what I'm sayin'?" He asked.

33

"Nigga, I know what it is, its mine! But I also know I just said I ain't rockin', so why we still on the phone?" I asked.

"True, aright then shawty, it is what it is, holla'." He said then he hung up the phone.

I shook my head as I tossed my phone onto the couch, then I went back into the bedroom.

After I dug the box back up, I pulled it out and punched in his birthday for the access code as he instructed. The box flipped open just as it had before revealing all of the money.

This time the aroma from all the money seemed to flush up into my face. I looked over it feeling mesmerized knowing that there was even more rows of it underneath the many rows on top.

"Concentrate Alisha, your man need you." I said as I slapped myself to regain my focus. I counted out twenty thousand dollars then I closed the case and carefully put it back. I carried all of the money over to the bed where I left the envelopes. Then I reached under the mattress to get the other envelope of money, which I also recounted.

Once I had all the money counted out, I band up the bundles by folding them over and stretching a rubber band around them before placing them into the envelope with the bubble wrap inside. I made sure the envelope was smooth and showing no impressions before I sealed it closed.

I didn't want to write on the envelope as I understood from watching forensics and cop shows, handwriting can be traced. So I grabbed the card I had gotten from the guy at the jail and went over to the computer where I created a label to type the address from the card onto.

I made sure that everything was accurate before printing the label, then I stretched it across the front of the envelope.

"Almost there baby." I said with a sigh as I looked at the envelope one last time.

34

Later I took it to the post office where I learned I needed two stamps because of its heft. I made the purchase and had them make it first class before I passed it off to them.

The entire time during the transaction I was praying that no one would be wise to the fact that there was money inside.

When I left the post office I decided to head to my folks house. I had never been away from Vinny this long and I missed him something terrible.

"Moooomy!" Vinny shouted when I pulled up to the house. He and my dad were out there playing with remote control cars.

"There goes my baaayby, oooh boy look at you!" I said as I got out of my car and opened my arms for him.

"Mommy, that's a girl song!" He said as he gave me a hug.

"Did I just sing it to a girl?" I asked once we let go.

"No, you sang it to me!" He said pointing at himself.

"Then it ain't no girl song then!" I said as I playfully pushed his head.

"Awww mommy!" He whined.

"Hey dad, where's ma?" I asked as I put Vinny in a headlock.

"Hey baby, she ran to the store to get somethings for dinner. Why you not at work?" He asked taking a seat in his chair with a look of relief written all over his face.

"Got some thing's going on dad." I said feeling a sadness coming over me.

"Vinny, why don't you go get us some ice cream?" My father asked.

"But gramma say it spoil my appotike" Vinny said as he watched his car roam through the yard.

"AppetiTe, and go do like granddaddy said." I demanded, realizing that my dad just wanted to talk to me alone.

"okay, hold this, don't let nobody take it." He said as he handed me the remote to the car.

"You can trust me!" I said with a chuckle.

"So your mother said Sean's been locked up, but you don't know why?" My dad started after Vinny got inside the house.

"Pretty much" I lied.

"Mmhmm, so what's going on with his bail?" My dad asked not sounding convinced.

"I don't know dad, I haven't heard anything about a bail." I said looking away.

"So now I'm stupid?" My dad asked.

"What?" I asked confused

"I'm supposed to believe you don't know what's going on with the man in your life?" He asked making that *'get the hell out of here'* face he always makes when he knew that a person was lying.

"Dad, it's under control." I said not wanting to feed him the details of how serious the situation was.

"Alisha, I understand that you don't want to tell me, he's your family, and I respect that. But don't let this thing get too big for you. We all need help some times." He said.

"He feels like he can handle it dad. I have to let him try. I can't go over his head without giving him a chance to do him." I explained.

"Respect." My dad said just as Vinny came busting out the house with the ice cream.

"Here granddaddy!' He said handing my dad one.

"Mommy, can you open this for me?" He asked holding his ice cream up to me.

"I told yall not to be eatin' that ice cream before dinner. Didn't I!" My mother hollered out of her window as she pulled up to the house.

"Vinny gave me this!" My father said as he pretended to hide the ice cream behind his back.

"Aww, granddaddy, you a tat-tell!" Vinny said looking over at my dad frowning. When he heard my mother's voice he dropped his ice cream on the ground like it was never in his hand.

"Blaming a *child*, you should be shame of your old ass self!" My mother said after she parked her car.

"Punish me then." He said as he walked over to her car.

"Boy hush it up and come get these groceries!" She said. We just laughed.

I stayed at my parents for dinner, then I had a talked with Vinny telling him that daddy had to take care of some business, so he may not be home for a little while. I hated lying to him, but I didn't want to tell him the truth. After our chat I decided to bring him home. I really missed him and I knew he'd rather be home with me, at least.

CHAPTER 4

About a week later I went back to see Sean. It had been very hard not having him home. Not being able to cuddle up with him, cook for him, nag him just to get on his nerves, or to have our family time that we tried to set aside at least once a week was starting to really take its toll on me. So I know that it was fucking with him the same way. For ten years its always been us, just us, only us. We were all we had to lean on, and that was by choice.

When I walked into the visitors room I saw him sitting at the table. He seemed to be staring into space as he played with his fingers.

"Baby, what's wrong?" I asked after I approached the table.

"Oh shit, what's up baby girl My mind was just somewhere else, I ain't even see you come in." He said happy as he stood to hug me. I didn't want to let him go, and he eagerly held me back.

"Damn I miss you ma." He said once we did let go.

"I miss you too." I replied sadly, ready to cry.

"Come on baby, don't do that to me up in here. I need you to be strong for daddy." He said as he took my hand into his.

"So what's new, what's going on now?" I asked to changing the subject in order to suppress my need to cry.

"yeah, I got some news baby, not bad, but jive fucked up, for now." He started.

"Okay." I replied encouraging him to continue.

"Well, since what I'm being accused of happened in Maryland, I'm being extradited back out Anne Arundel County. But, that's being delayed because they claim they shipped my paperwork to Seven Locks out Moco (Montgomery County, Maryland), with some nigga that's got my same name, so they gotta get that straight first." Sean said sounding pissed off.

"Delayed, just like those cops said." I replied as I recalled the day I heard the cops plotting in the waiting area.

"I know right, tell me something, you remember hearin' any names in that convo?' He asked.

"Uhm, the one cop kept sayin' the other cops name, uh... It started with a D." I said trying to think.

"Davis, Douglas, Dennis, Donald's..." Sean asked trying to help jog my memory.

"Daniels!" I exclaimed drawing the attention of a couple people who were within earshot.

"Aright baby, calm down. Hmm, Daniels huh, okay." Sean said as a sick smile crept upon his face.

"Young, please get that crazy ass look off your face." I said I said with a raised eyebrow.

"What, I'm smilin', I can't smile now?" He asked with a chuckle.

"Nigga, not like that." I replied creeped out.

"Anyway, we ain't got much time left, how's Vinny?" He asked as he seemed to shake the crazy off.

"He's good, just missing you." I replied.

"I miss yall too. I can barely sleep in here because I can't hold you or smell you. I can't hear you half snore half talk in your sleep. I been worried as shit about you havin' one of your bad dreams and I'm not there." He said.

My only reply were the tears that fell from my eyes.

"You're my everything Alisha, even though we fuss and argue, I wouldn't change being your man for the world." He said.

39

"I wouldn't change it either Sean. I love and miss you too. It's hard being in our bed without you." I said as more tears found their way to my eyes.

"I know baby, but right now ain't the time to get weak. I need you to be strong, I need you to use this time to show us what you made of. That survivor woman I fell in love with, that me and Vinny need right now. I know it's hard, and your heart hurts, but it ain't ova, I promise you. So don't let that be why you cryin'." He said as he lift my chin to have me look into his eyes.

"It's just hard Sean." I sobbed.

"I know I'm puttin' a lot of stress on us right now, but I just need you to have faith in me, and know, I'ma do all I can to make it back to you. I just need you to trust me." He said.

"Okay." I replied.

That night I lie in bed staring up at the ceiling as I listened to the rain fall. On nights like this, Sean and I use to hold hands in bed until we fell asleep. Even if we were angry with one another, the rain for some reason would bring peace between us. I missed the hell out of that man. Eventually I curled up with his pillow and went to sleep.

CHAPTER 5

Three weeks had passed before they were able to get Sean's paperwork straight. He was to be extradited the day after tomorrow. He asked me to come see him today because he didn't like the idea of me traveling all the way out to Anne Arundel County alone. But he was crazy in the head if he thought I wouldn't make that trip. I'd go to the ends of the Earth to be with him.

He did assure me that his lawyer had a fool proof plan and that all he needed was to get this ball rolling. With that being the case, he really couldn't wait to be extradited, the sooner the better as far as he was concerned.

Vinny made it no secret that he missed his father. Even though he was only four he was hip to a lot more than we gave him credit for. Having never gone so long without his dad, it was really taking a toll on him as well.

I did my best to reassure him that everything was okay, but it didn't help that he caught me crying more than once. I'm sure this did something unspeakable to his psyche. What, I have no idea.

I requested a personal day off from work and arranged it so that my parents would pick Vinny up after school so that I could use the extra hours to get beautified. I wanted to give Sean a pic to take with him to Anne Arundel until I could make it up there to see him. I had a hair and nails appointment set . But first I wanted to go cop an outfit that he'd never seen before, and some more of the body spray and lotion that he liked on me. I was going to do it up for him.

When I left the apartment, I walked through the parking lot to my car and noticed a couple of guys walking towards me. Paying them no mind I continued for my car.

"What's up cutie, how you doin?" The younger one asked.

"I'm good." I replied disinterested as I kept walking.

"I see that shit, so whats ya name?" He asked as they kept approaching.

"Nah, I'm good slim, go 'head about your business." I said mugging him.

"You are my business, and I'm 'bout to be all about you." He slicked. I turned around to look at him like he was crazy, that's when I noticed a black sack in his friends' hand.

"Shit!" I said as I took off running.

They were too close for me to get into my car safely so I ran passed my car attempting to run for the street where I knew the hustlers were.

"Man, get that bitch!" I heard the other older guy shout.

"Come on man, calm down! She ain't that fast!" The younger guy said as he was catching up to me.

I turned around and with all my might I swung on him punching him in the face. He belted over holding his eye and I kept beating him in the face. He was covering his face as he took the hits. I started really giving it to him in hopes that it would slow him down so that I could get away. The older guy, who was much bigger struggled to catch up with us. However, I knew that eventually he would so I kneed the younger one in the dick and turned to run again.

"Nigga, did you just let a girl whup your bitchass?" I heard the bigger one ask sounding as though he were out of breath.

"Nigga fuck you, I don't hit women!" The younger one exclaimed.

"Nigga, if a bitch hittin' you like a nigga, you supposed to knock that ass out. Fuck the bullshit, go get that fuckin bitch!" The older one shouted between breaths.

I ran as fast as I could, but it wasn't fast enough. The younger one caught me and held my arms down like he as arresting me. The older fatter one came and slipped the black case over my head and from there I was lift up over someone's shoulder, kicking and yelling.

42

After being placed in what I could only imagine to be a vehicle, I heard a door slide close, and moments later we were moving.

'"What the *FUCK*!" I shouted

I couldn't believe that I was being kidnapped again! But for what this time, and by who? I don't have shit, I don't know shit. Then it struck me, *'Someone must've found out about all of Sean's money. But fuckin how? Did I send it to the wrong address? Did Goldberg set Sean up?'* My mind flashed over every possible scenario but I couldn't make full sense out of any of them.

The vehicle drove around for what felt like a very long time before it came to a halt. I felt it back up then stop. A few minutes later I heard the door slide open, and I was dragged by my feet to the other side until whoever it was could reach me. That's when I was put over a shoulder and carried off.

I was carried up what felt like two flight of stairs before I heard a door open and then close.

"Man, I can't just sit her down 'cause she goin start fightin', what you want me to do? We got some shit to knock her out?" I heard the younger one's voice ask.

"Yeah nigga, your fuckin fist. Still can't believe *you*, a grown ass man got yo ass whupped by a fucking bitch. You lost all your points with me dog, after this job, I don't got me fuckin wit you no more." The older one said.

"Nigga fuck you. What the fuck jo, we tying her up or what?" The younger one asked sounding impatient

"Nah, we goin let her roam the apartment in hopes that she'll find something incriminating that'll send us to jail for life. *yeah* nigga we tying her the fuck up. Let me hit the lights first." The older guy said.

That's when I felt myself being taken off the shoulder and sat in a chair.

"Start wit her feet first so she can't run." The older guy said as someone lift the sack over my ankles.

"I'll hold her, you do this." Said the older guy while his hands gripped my arms tightly.

Once my feet were tied they lift the sack around my waist and tied the rope around my waist and around and between my wrists.

"She good now, go get the tape for her mouth. I can tell this bitch got a mouth that's goin make me wanna slap the shit out of her." The older guy said as they took the sack off of me completely.

The room was dark with the exception of the light from the TV and computer which were on opposites sides of the room. I watched Jake and the fat man look around in different places for the tape.

"So what the fuck is all this for?" I decided to ask. I figured hell, they were gonna do what they were gonna do whether I bitched or not, so fuck it.

"What?" The fat one shot at me as though he couldn't believe I had the nerve to speak.

"Did I stutter? Why the fuck yall kidnap me?" I asked giving up straight attitude.

"Bitch, you talking shit *and* you tied up. Where the fuck they do that at? Your life in is my hands, you don't ask questions, you submit!" The fat man said as he walked over to me.

"Yeah, anyway. Y'all kidnapped *me*, so yall gotta plan to do what yall goin do whether I'm quiet or not. I just wanna know what it is" I said still spittin' shit.

"You got a smart ass muhfuckin mouth. Who the fuck you think you is shawty?" The older one said getting in my face.

"I'm *somebody*, or I wouldn't be here right now, am I right?" I asked rocking my head.

The Power Of Love 2 Short Stories by Nikida Bellezza

"I swear to god i'ma end up fuckin this bitch up. Nigga get that tape off the early jo, get that muthafuckin tape before I fuck this bitch up!" The older guy said as he walked away.

"Got it." The younger one said holding up some duct tape.

"Bet, hurry up and gag that bitch!" The older one said.

The younger one took out a knife and cut a strip of tape off the roll before walking over to me. I shook my head as he put it over my lips.

"Thank you, peace and fuckin quiet!" The older one shouted.

"Not wit'chu' yellin' like that cuz." The younger one said with a chuckle.

"Awww nigga shut yo *'got beat by a woman ass up!'* " The older one said.

I shook my head in anger, fear and sadness as I began to think about Sean being in the waiting room, waiting for me to walk through the doors, these were the thoughts that brought tears to my eyes.

CHAPTER 6

I saw the sun rise and set, which served as my only real indication that a day had passed. Well, outside of the kidnappers taking random naps after stuffing their faces with pizza and carryout.

They never asked me if I were hungry or thirsty, nor did they seem to care if I needed to use the bathroom. Truth be told, I really didn't have an appetite, nor did I want to fall asleep as I felt that I needed to be conscious just in case a name, or *"the plan"* slipped out of one of their mouths.

Most of the time, they seemed to forget that I was even here. So I reasoned that whatever the plan was, they needed me alive for it, at least for now.

Seeing how it had been at least twenty-four hours since I last used the restroom, the urge to do so was starting to make *'ride or die'* demands on me. I rocked back in forth in the chair attempting to hold it, while humming to get their attention.

"Aye, see what the fuck goin on wit her!" The older one said to the younger one. I guess the website he was on was just too intriguing to turn away from.

"Man, aright. Whats wrong wit' yo ass now slim? What you hungry?" The younger one said as he approached me.

I rolled my eyes at him, then jerked my head towards my lap so that he would notice that I was rocking back and forth.

"Oh shit, she ga' go to the bathroom!" The younger one said to the older one.

"Damn bitch, you on your period?" The older one yelled across the room at me. I rolled my eyes and jerked my head at him to show my attitude.

46

"Is that a fuckin yes or no, you wastin' time, I ain't the one that's got to piss." He said. I rolled my eyes again and shook my head.

"Aright, go head and take her to the bathroom." The older one said throwing a dismissive gesture towards me with his arm.

"How I'm s'pose to do that? She tied the fuck up?" The younger one said.

"You gonna have to wipe her." The older one said with a chuckle.

I hummed my retort as I shook my head wildly. That wasn't even about to be the plan.

"Oh, I can do that." He said looking down at me. I mugged him as I hummed a 'hell no.'

"Look, its either that, or you don't get wiped at all, its smooth up to you shawty." The older one said with a dirty man chuckle.

I shook my head trying to convince myself to just go ahead and let it flow. I was not about to let this lil nigga feel on me.

"Oh, so I guess you goin piss yourself then huh?" The younger one said taunting me.

I rolled my eyes and turned my head away from him.

"Don't go chasin' water falls, I know you gotta go to the bathroom, either let me wipe that coochie or piss all over yourself, to me it don't matter at all." He said singing and dancing.

"Nigga you stupid as shit." The older one said laughing.

"Hmm, you holdin' in that pee huh, that thang must be tight. You got a tight pussy? Mmh, I might have to see what's good wit' it." He said still taunting me.

I looked over at him and gritted on him hard (to give disrespectful look). He had me fucked all the way up if he thought he was gonna take it without a fight from me, tied up or not.

"Aye, slim, come look at this fuckin shit!' Exclaimed the older guy sounding distressed.

47

"Nah nigga, I'm bout to see what this pussy like." He said as he slipped his hand between my legs. I squeezed my thighs tight to prevent him from moving up any further.

"Nah nigga, you need to come see this shit, early!" The big one said sounding worried.

"yeah, make sure you squeeze that pussy for me just like that." He said before hanging his tongue out his mouth like a hungry dog.

If I didn't have this tape over my mouth I would've spit in his face. He smiled at me then he walked over to join the other guy at the computer.

"Fuck is up nigga?" He asked leaning in to see the screen.

"This shit, this muthafucka made a fuckin video collage" The older guy said pointing at the screen.

"From jail? Of what, all the dicks goin in and out of his faggy ass?" The younger guy replied with a chuckle.

"Nigga look again." The older guy said as he stood to his feet to let the younger guy sit down.

"*You.. don't.. want... that... beef...* Aww shit nigga, that's my folks house!' The younger guy exclaimed as he stood to his feet after reading the words that appeared across the screen.

"No shit bitch, that's my mother, my niece, my house..." The older guy said sounding like he wanted to cry.

"That's my son." The younger guy said as I saw the words '*DO YOU*?' Stretch across the screen in bold letters.

"Oh fuck nah! Fuck that shit, fuck them cops, they can keep them forty g's" The younger guy said as he paced the room in a panic.

The Power Of Love 2 Short Stories by Nikida Bellezza

"Nigga, you walkin' holes in this floor, untie that bitch and let her fuckin go!" The older guy shouted.

"Man, my head fucked up man. Young, my son though? How the fuck he get to my lil youngin'?!" The younger one said.

"Man fuck what you talkin bout, I'm untying this shit and I'm out!" The older guy said as he ran over to me. He turned me around in my chair and started untying me.

"Look shawty, this was just business, tell cuz we let you go. Tell him we ain't know what the fuck it was all about. Tell him we were hired by some cops!" The older one said as he furiously worked to untie me.

"Please slim, please, I'm sorry for touching you, and talkin shit. I'm so sorry. Tell cuz it was all a misunderstanding, and we can work that shit off. If he want us, he got us." The younger one said.

I shook my head as I began to wonder, just who in the hell Sean really was in these streets.

"Shawty, again, I'm so sorry. If you wanna hit me or whateva, I understand." The older one said once my hands were free.

"Dog, my son, them fuckin cops set us the fuck up! Whole time they knew who this nigga was and how he get down!" The younger one exclaimed still fucked up.

"Man, fuck all that, let's just get her untied and back home, then we ghost!" The older one said as he started untying my ankles.

"Yeah, yeah, I'm outta here, fuck DC!" The younger one proclaimed.

"Fuck DC? Nigga yo bitchass lived here for what, all of two minutes? Get the fuck outta here!" The older one said

"Man, I'm from right off Southern ave, DC is right across the fuckin street. Benning road is down the street. I been here all my life!" The younger one exclaimed

"Maryland ass niggas, I swear." The older one mumbled as he shook his head.

"Man fuck that shit let's roll!' The younger one said.

Once I was free I stood to my feet and attempted to ease the tape off my mouth, but it hurt like hell.

"Come on, this way to the bathroom" the older one said guiding me.

I followed him over then I went inside and slammed the door closed before locking it.

Then I raised my skirt, forced my panties down and hovered.

I moaned like crazy as my body was finally able to release the pressure.

Afterwords I cleaned up, washed my hands and went for a second attempt to get the tape off.

This time I tried to use water, but that didn't help either. I stared at myself in the mirror as I tried to prepare myself for the next step that lingered in my thoughts.

'Please Lord, don't let me tear my skin off.' I thought to myself as I shook my head.

I gave one last time I attempt to ease the tape off and it hurt like shit. I was able to will myself to take it, and made it as far as where my nose lined up with my lips, but it got too painful and I just couldn't take it anymore. So, I took a deep breath and snatched the rest off.

Too scared to look at my face right away, I closed my eyes. When I opened them, I looked down at the tape and saw single short strands of hair on it.

"What the fuck, I got hair on my face?!" I heard my hoarse voice exclaim as I looked up in the mirror.

That's when I saw that my bottom lip and the skin beside my lips had small cuts on them that were bleeding from the tape being snatched. I looked up into my eyes to see that they were bloodshot red from being so sleepy, and my hair looked a hot ass mess. I looked terrible, but a lot of it was the stress of not having Sean around.

We didn't always see eye to eye, but he was a part of my spirit, and my being knew that he was missing, and man was it hard to go on without him.

I left the bathroom and saw the two goof balls leaning against the wall looking pitiful. I shook my head at them before walking towards the door.

"Let's go." I said in my new found hoarse voice. They jumped off the wall and followed me over to the door. We walked down the steps and out to a big Brown van, that was identical to the van from the show "Who's The Boss."

We all climbed inside, me and the older guy in the front, and the younger one in the back.

It was interesting how quiet they were during the ride back to my house. After all the taunting and shit talking they were doing, I just knew they had balls of solid steel.

As for me, my silence came from an array of feelings as my nerves were screaming at the top of their lungs. Truth is I was scared to death the entire time, there were moments when I had a relapse of the fear I felt while I was held in Mr. McGills basement. However, I wasn't even about to let them know scared I actually was. I made a promise to Sean and myself a long time ago, never show fear. Sean was real big on street life rules, as he spout them at me constantly...

'Neva' let a nigga know he got what you need, he can know that he got what you want, but only if you got what he need in return.' .. 'Never show a nigga fear, if he weak, and you real, your confidence can convince him that the gun he himself loaded is empty, ...if he a real nigga, he ain't comin' at you with bullshit, so be prepared to battle if you don't got what you owe, but never be

scared, fate is fate."

Recalling Sean's random life speeches in my head almost brought a tear to my eyes, GOD I missed that man.

"Look, I can't apologize enough. We were workin' for some cops that paid us forty g's to do this. And you know, to some bum ass niggas, that's a nice chunk of change." The older guy said breaking the silence.

"That don't excuse shit. It's hard out here for erybody, but whatever, who were the cops?" I asked fronting like I wasn't still shaken up.

"No doubt, no excuse. They're names are Fred Wenarsky and Benjamin Daniels." The younger one called from the back.

'There go that dam name again.' I thought to myself.

When we pulled into my parking lot, he stopped the van in front of where they picked me up then turned to look at me.

"Look, we already spent some of the money, but here is what we have left." The older one said as he reached into the glove compartment and grabbed the stacks of money.

"Keep it" I said as I popped the door handle to open the door.

"Nah, please, give it to him. Please." The older one urged.

"He ain't goin want that." I said before hopping out of the van.

When I got to the sidewalk they pulled off.

I quickly walked over to my building, I wanted to run inside and lock the door behind me.

Suddenly I was feeling very vulnerable and even more afraid. I could feel the tears burning their way to my eyes, but I tried my best to suppress them as I made my way to the building.

Before I got to the entrance, I saw my neighbor Jack walk out of the building twirling his car keys without a care in the world. When he saw me he broke into a wide grin.

"Alisha, hey, I found your purse in the street under my truck. I ain't been able to catch up with you to get it back to you. Hang on, I'll run and get it now for you now." Jack said before turning to head back into the building.

"Jack!" I said before bursting into tears. From out of nowhere I began to cry hard and uncontrollably.

"Alisha, what's going on, what's wrong?" Jack asked as he walked back over to me and put his arms around me. I was crying too hard to answer him.

"Baby I thought you were going to start the car.. Alisha? Oh my gawd Jacki what's the matter?" His wife Gina said after stepping outside.

"I don't know she just started crying, take her in the house, let me check around." He said.

"Okay, come on baby. It's okay, it's gonna be alright." Gina said as she guided me into the building. We went into her apartment and sat on the couch.

"Whatever it is God is going to take care of it. God will see you through." Gina said as she rubbed my shoulder.

"I need to use the phone." I said between sobs.

"Of course honey, here." She said handing me her house phone. I had to wipe my eyes several times to see the buttons clearly. Once I did I pressed in the numbers.

"I'll give you some privacy." Gina said before getting up to leave

"HELLO? HELLO?" I heard my mom's voice exclaim.

"Ma, it's me!" I said crying more.

53

"Oh Lord, thank you Jesus, hallelujah! Pete she's on the phone!" My mother shouted.

"HELLO, ALISHA?" My dad exclaimed after picking up another phone in the house.

"Yes daddy, it's me!" I cried.

"Where are you?!" My mother asked.

"I'm home, I'm at my neighbors apartment now." I said seconds later I heard one of the lines click.

"Okay baby we are on the way stay there... *PETE WAIT FOR ME!!*" I heard my mother shout before hanging up the phone.

"Hey lady, Jack found this under his truck a couple days ago. Forgive us, when we couldn't get in contact with you, so we got worried and called your parents from your cell." She said as she handed me back my purse.

"Thank you." I said. It had totally slipped my mind that I dropped my purse while beating on the younger of the two guys who kidnapped me.

"So do you want anything to eat or drink?" Gina asked in her best attempt to be a good hostess.

"No, but can I just wait here for my parents?" I asked.

"Of course. You wanna go lay down, or you good here?" She asked.

"I'm good." I said. She looked at me for a second then she came and sat next to me and put her arms around me.

Gina and Jack were the only couple in our building that we fucked with. They had us by a couple years, but they were cool and down to Earth people. Ready to help you and quick to side with you when it came to confrontation.

54

The Power Of Love 2 Short Stories by Nikida Bellezza

Gina was what I considered to be an 'Earth Sista', she wore her hair natural and only wore earth tone makeup. She was in touch with her afro centric roots, but had no problem going South East on that ass if you ever got her fucked up.

Jack was cool too, he was chill, you can tell he use to get his hands dirty once upon a time, but now he was laid back and mellow. He wasn't as into the roots thing as Gina, but you could tell he adored her and all that she was about.

"Hey, her car and windows to her place look okay, how she doin?" Jack asked as he walked into the apartment.

"Shhh, let her rest some." I heard Gina whisper.

"Okay baby, I'll be in the room." Jack whispered back before leaving the room.

Once he was gone Gina began humming a soft tune. I couldn't make out the actual words, but I knew that it was some gospel song.

She had a very nice singing voice, and at the moment it was putting me to sleep. Fifteen minutes later I was awakened by the sound of their house phone.

I jumped up hoping that it was my parents. I was beginning to feel like a lost child who desperately wanted to get home to the safety of their parents.

"Hello? Oh yes ma'am she is right here, one moment please." I heard Gina say just before handing me the phone.

"Hello?" I nearly shouted.

"Baby we're outside" My mother exclaimed.

"okay, I'm coming out." I said then I ended the call.

"Gina thank you so much for having my back the way you do. I so appreciate you and Jack.!" I said giving her a hug.

"Let me tell you something sista, that's what we are supposed to do. Black women need to be there for each other, we need to strengthen ourselves because through us our families will find their strength. It is my pleasure to be there for you, anytime!" She said hugging me back.

I left their apartment and ran down the stairs to see my parents standing on the sidewalk with Vinny.

"MOMMY!" Vinny screamed. I ran over and swooped him up. The tears came flooding to my eyes, it wasn't until that moment that I felt like I was back home. My parents both hugged me while I was holding Vinny. We stood out there hugging each other for what could have been an eternity. Whatever length of time it was, it didn't matter, it could've very well been forever and it wouldn't have bothered us at all.

Eventually we let go and my parents came up to my apartment to help me gather some clothes and things, then they took me and Vinny home with them. There I gave them subtle details about the kidnapping, leaving Sean out of it, but the way my father looked at me, I could tell that he knew it had something to do with Sean, but being happy to have me back home, he never mentioned his suspicions.

CHAPTER 7

That night after having the long talk with my parents about what happened to me, I lie in my old bed and allowed my mind to retrace the events that occurred over the last forty-eight hours. That's when I began to realize just how serious this situation with Sean really is.

I also began to seriously wonder WHO Sean really was.

Where'd he get all the money, why did he have that guy Goldberg's number on standby, and how did he know what conversation I'd have with Goldberg when he answered the phone. And I guess most importantly, if he was locked up, how did he find out who the kidnappers were, where did he get the pictures to make the collage, and how in the hell did he make the collage from a cell?

Sean was always quiet about his street life, and to my knowledge he gave up that life years ago. He knew A LOT of people, but in front of me, his conversations were always short and very causal. He never introduced me to anyone, but he'd stand there and kick it for a few seconds with his arm around me or holding my hand, and the person would never really acknowledge me. I used to get mad about it, but eventually I stopped caring because it became common, especially when his response was always *'if I need you to know somebody, you will.'* then he'd add *'just never forget a face.'*

By now he should've been in Ann Arundel County, awaiting to hear the next steps in his case. I missed him terribly, but I was also afraid now as I realized Sean kept me out of the loop about so many things.

I understood that it was for my safety, but It seemed as though every aspect of his life that I didn't know about was being revealed in dangerous ways.

I loved Sean endlessly, but I couldn't help but worry about what the exposure of the next part of his life had in store for me.

I closed my eyes trying to force my mind to stop, but the barrage of thoughts had my full attention thusly having full control. However, my thoughts were soon interrupted by the piercing sound of my cell phone ringing. The noise was quite startling in the depths of silence.

I sat up and grabbed my phone off the night stand noting by the ring tone that the person was calling from a number that wasn't programmed in my phone.

"What the fuck?" I asked after seeing that a number with area code 667 was flashing across the screen.

"Please God, no more trouble." I said before pushing the answer button.

"Hello?" I asked.

"Baby girl, it's me." I heard Sean's voice say

"Oh my gawd, Sean!' I exclaimed excited and relieved to hear his voice.

"Yeah, baby. One of the guards is my mans, so he lettin' me use this cell. But fuck all that, how are you, are you okay?" He asked all in one breath.

"No Sean, I'm not okay, my life is fucked up! How could you leave me out here like this?!" I asked crying.

"I'm sorry baby girl I fucked up, I left you out there unprotected. I can't stop shit from happenin', I can only fix it when it do." He said after a pause.

"Sean, I'm scared. I'm at my parents house because I don't want to be alone. I'm a grown woman, but I feel like a little girl that needs her daddy." I said.

"I know baby, I know you need me, I need you too. I promise you daddy gonna fix it. Then me you and Vinny are dippin' out." Sean said.

I didn't reply, I just sobbed into the phone.

"Baby girl, I gotta ask you a question tho." He said.

"What?" I asked.

"Did they do anything to you?" He asked

"They tied me up and put tape on my mouth, and the younger one tried to touch me." I recalled.

"Where?" He asked.

"Between my legs." I answered knowing that he would get angry.

"Hmph, yeah okay." He replied upset.

"Sean?" I asked.

"Yes baby?" He said.

"Are you coming home to me?" I asked.

"Dead, or Alive." He replied confidently.

"Alive please." I responded.

"You got it." He assured.

"So how long before we know what's going on?" I inquired after a brief silence.

"I already know what's going on" he answered nonchalantly

"Well I don't! I mean don't you think you kept me out the loop long enough? I'm out here in the middle of all your shit, and you takin' it all in stride! Am I your fuckin girl or am I a pawn?! I asked very upset.

"You're my wife, and I never meant for shit to go down like it did." He replied calmly.

"But it did! Them niggas coulda' raped me Sean, they coulda' killed me, then what?!" I exclaimed.

He didn't respond right away, instead I heard him breath in deeply.

"Yeah man, I'm good... yeah dog, go head man." I heard him say in the background.

"Alisha, I fucked up, and I failed you. But ask yourself this question, if my life is all you feel it is, and I'm not denying or confirming anything, but if you think I'm livin' that type of life, you know I ain't just start livin' it, which means, it's been *this* the whole time. And with you *just* finding out, wouldn't you say I've been on my job as your protector?" He asked calmly

"And what about now Sean, I need you now." I said.

"I know baby girl, and I'm working on gettin' home to you and Vinny as fast as I can. Don't think I'm chillin', or that I'm thinking shit sweet. Trust me, business is being handled on the daily." He said.

"Okay." I replied giving up. I felt as though he didn't understand my plight and it was frustrating me.

"Lisha, baby, you are my whole life. When I met you at Jayjo's cookout, and you were wearing that red hobo shirt, them short pants and them red chucks, I was like, she a bama, but she pretty as shit. I knew that day, that you were goin be my wife. You were sittin' at the table talkin to my man Speedy's lil sister. I stared at you for a minute, when you finally looked up, you smiled and looked away, fakin' that shy shit." He said.

"Nigga whateva, neva' was I eva' a bama! And I was shy, but I saw you starin' at me the whole time." I said with a chuckle.

"I know you did, I wanted you too see me. Point is, you were the girl I wanted, and now you're the woman I need. Don't second guess me, and don't second guess us. You don't always need to know everything, sometimes its better when you don't. And sometimes the shit is just so irrelevant, but something I need you to always know is that no matter what it is, I got you, okay?" He asked.

"Okay Sean." I replied feeling a little better.

"I love you Alisha. He said

"I love you too." I replied.

"Let me get off this phone. I'ma try to hit you again tomorrow. If not it will be soon, okay?" He said.

"Okay." I answered.

CHAPTER 8

I spent the next three and a half weeks at my parents, only going home to get clothes and toys for Vinny and I. I never realized how much more secure Sean always made me feel until he was no longer physically with me. I wasn't sure if that was a good or bad thing. He called and spoke with me and Vinny at least twice a week. When Vinny would ask where he was, he told him that he had to take care of some business out of town and that he would be home as soon as he could. We don't know if Vinny bought it, but by being able to speak to Sean, his spirits were lifted some, and that was good enough for now because, that was all we had.

One evening when I came to my parents home after work I walked into the house to see my mom sitting on the edge of the couch watching the news.

"Hey ma, why you sitting like you're about to hop inside the TV?" I asked as I sat my purse in my dad's lazy-boy.

"Girl, there's this whole scandal surrounding this case. These cops had been tampering with an inmates paperwork sending it all over from Maryland to Virginia, then they hired kidnappers to hold the inmates girlfriend hostage. Chile, there was even a death threat sent to the inmates lawyer, girl this is crazy! This like an episode straight out of a movie" She exclaimed.

"What?" I asked as I turned my attention to the TV. That's when I saw the cop Daniels and the other cop's pictures on the side of the screen.

"Oh my GAWD!" I shouted.

"What, what, you know them?" My mother asked exclaimed standing up.

"Shhh, ma, turn it up" I said as I sat in the lazy-boy.

"The two officers who both plead guilty to tampering and conspiring the kidnapping are being held without bond. For their cooperation the two hired kidnappers will serve lighter sentences. As for the murder case that inspired all of this, the judge ruled just a few hours ago that the case has to be thrown out. The young man accused of murder will walk out of Jennifer Road Detention Center, a free man." The news anchor reported.

"Ma, oh my gawd ma, do you know what this means?" I screamed as I jumped to my feet.

"*What,* what?" She asked jumping up as well.

"*SEAN IS FREE! HE'S COMING HOME*!' I shouted which brought my dad and Vinny into the room.

"What's going on in here?" My dad asked.

"That was about Sean?!" My mother asked confused. I forgot I never told them that he was wanted for murder.

"Yes, I have to go get him!" I exclaimed as I ripped my purse open to get my keys out.

"I don't think so." My father said sternly.

"What you mean... Oh my gawd!" I screamed after turning around to see Sean walking up the side walk.

When he saw me burst out of the house he grew the widest smile across his face. I ran down the steps and into his arms nearly knocking him over.

"Baby Girl!' He said as he held me lifting me off my feet.

"Oh my gawd, I was on my way to get you! I just saw it on the news!" I said still holding onto him for dear life.

"The news is only news for the folks that don't already know. All that you see on there already happened." He explained.

"I don't care, you're home now and that's all I need!" I said.

"Daddy!' Vinny yelled as he came running out of the house. I let go of Sean so that Vinny could get his turn.

"Oh shit, my lil man. Lookin' like you try become daddy's big man!" Sean said taking Vinny up into his arms.

"I miss you!' Vinny said

"Aww man, I missed you too. But daddy back now, and he ain't goin nowhere!' Sean said looking at me as he mouthed the words 'I promise.'

CHAPTER 9

A few days later I got a call from the D.A. who wanted me to come in for questioning about my kidnapping. Sean offered to go with me but I wanted him to keep far away from the judicial system, no jinx shit over here.

When I got to the District Attorney's office, I found out where I needed to go and was directed there. I walked right by the two men who had kidnapped me, they were in prison suits handcuffed to one another. The younger one had a bandage wrapped around his wrist covering the area where his hand used to be. I found that quite odd but I opted not to stare too long as I didn't want to make eye contact with them. I just wanted to get in here and get out a quickly as possible.

After fifteen minutes of waiting, I was called into the office where they asked me a series of questions, about the kidnapping. Like what happened while I was held captive, was there a ransom paid, and what caused them to let me go? I answered the questions to the best of my ability without linking anything to Sean. Then they had me sign some paperwork and allowed me to go.

Once the questioning was over I returned home to see Sean and Vinny in the living room playing Sean's game.

"Hey baby, lil man, let daddy talk to mommy real quick, go play in your room." Sean said.

"okay, hi mommy, bye mommy!' Vinny said before running back to his room.

"Hey baby." I said with a chuckle as I sat next to Sean on the couch.

"So how'd it go?" He asked as he dropped his controller on the table.

"It was okay, they asked me everything I thought they would." I said.

"So you were good?" He asked.

"Yeah, pretty much. Oh, I saw the guys who kidnapped me, down there too." I said.

"Oh yeah." He replied uninterested.

"yeah, the younger one is missing a hand." I said.

"Damn." Sean replied, again uninterested.

"Right, it's the same hand he touched me with." I added, fishing.

"That's fucked up, I guess Karma really is a bitch." Sean said as he stood to stretch.

"No doubt, it's got cops confessing, cases being thrown out, and niggas losing hands." I said as I followed him into the kitchen.

"How 'bout that?" He asked going into the refrigerator for some juice.

"Nigga, Who *ARE* you?" I asked with a chuckle.

"De'Sean Taylor." He replied casually.

"That's all I need to know?" I asked now with my hands on my hips

"Trust me." He said as he walked up on me, kissed my lips and walked away.

THE END

Closure

A Nikida Bellezza Short

"Mommy NO!!" I screamed before waking up in a cold sweat. I shook my head as I leaned back against my headboard bringing my knees to my chest. Moments later my grandmother rushed into my room and flicked on the lights.

"You had the dream again?" She asked with the most worried look on her face. Still shaken, I nodded my head yes as the tears began to gather in my eyes.

She came and sat next to me and took me into her arms.

"It will get better Quinn, I promise you honey, it won't always be like this." My grandmother assured me as she cradled me in her arms.

"Grandma, it's been six years, and the dream is still so real. Why does my mind keep replaying it over and over? Why won't it let me forget?" I asked crying.

"Because it's attached to love. You will never forget your parents, and you will never forget the last day of their lives. I'm just so sorry you had to be a witness to it all." My grandmother said.

I shook my head as more tears found their way to my eyes. I remembered everything as though it were just yesterday..

Six Years Earlier

"Nigga fuck you, pussy ass nigga! Aww don't try to bargain now muthafucka!"

**BAP BAP BAP BAP*

"What's going on?" I asked as I jumped out of bed taking my headphones off. I walked into the living room and saw my mother sprawled on the floor with holes in her face.

"Mommy, No!" I screamed.

"Quinn, no, baby get out of here!' My father shouted in tears. That's when I noticed the man standing across the room in all black holding a gun.

The Power Of Love 2 Short Stories by Nikida Bellezza

"Awww shit, you gotta daughter too?! How old?" He asked my dad as he rubbed his private.

"Please, no, you took my wife, just kill me. I got $100,000 cash in a safe behind that picture. The combination is 25-33-10 please, kill me, take it and go. Please!" My father begged on his knees.

"Daddy, what's happening?" I asked scared to death.

"Quinn, baby, I made a mistake, please baby girl, just go. Forget everything you see here." My dad said crying, which I had never seen in my entire life. The man tilted his head at my dad like he were confused.

"Nigga, you done calling the shots, and I ain't got no mercy for you or your family bitch!" The man said as he walked over to me and choked me down to the floor.

"Time to pay the piper bitch, now watch her take this pipe!" He said as he snatched up my night gown and ripped my panties off.

"Please, PLEASE! She's innocent, please!" My dad screamed. I struggled under him until he jabbed himself inside me. I screamed out in excruciating pain.

"Awww shit, she a virgin, jackpot!" The guy said looking at my dad as he kept pounding me.

My dad ran over to jump on him but took a bullet to the forehead on the way. He dropped to the floor and didn't move.

I screamed and cried from the pain of being raped and from losing my parents.

Once he was done violating me he kissed me, then he got up and ran. I lie there on the floor wanting to die. By the time the police found me I had lapsed into a coma.

It was later that I discovered that I had become pregnant that night. Child Social Services sent me to live with my grandmother in North Carolina.

My grandmother was a very religious woman and wouldn't hear of me getting rid of the baby.

Instead she helped me raise him, as she reasoned, everything happens for a reason, and everybody deserves a chance. I actually did grow to love him, although it took time to separate his connection with his father whom I saw as a monster.

Present Day

Later that day as I sat on the porch watching my son Quinton play with his best friend Ronald. I sipped on my grandmother's prize winning iced tea and let my mind wonder into the fairytale escape I often used to ease my emotions.

"Quinn, honey, there's something I need to tell you. I think it's time." She said as she sat next to me. She was holding on to a stack of mail and other papers.

"What is it grandma?" I asked as I sat up.

"About a year after your parents passed, I started receiving checks in the mail. One addressed to me for $2,000, and one addressed to you for $5,000. They'd come every few months." She began.

"But from who?" I asked confused. We never really communicated with other family members, and my dad's job sucked, at least he always used to say that so that couldnt've been the source of the money either.

"I don't know honey. Here are the letters, look through them." She said handing them to me.

"I opened a bank account for you and have been depositing your checks for you." She continued.

I looked at the letter which didn't say anything at all, it only had an address from where it was sent.

"But, I don't understand. Who would be sending us all of this money?" I asked looking back up at my grandmother.

"I don't know dear, that's always been the mystery. Here is your account information and your bank card. Now that you are twenty-two, I feel that you are ready to be responsible for your own finances." She said.

"Oh my gawd!" I said as my eyes zeroed in on the amount of money in my account.

"Use it wisely honey, I don't know if or when the money will stop coming." She said with a pat on my shoulder before standing on her feet to leave.

"Of course grandma, of course." I said still looking at the money.

"I'm going to start supper. Get him washed up in about half an hour." She said as she entered the house.

"Yes ma'am." I said. I sat back in my seat and looked out at the neighborhood as a million thoughts shot through my mind. With one in particular that I just could not shake. *Who was sending this money, and why?*

I looked down at the address of the sender again and noted that it was mailed from Brandywine, Maryland. When my parents were alive we lived deep in Upper Marlboro, Maryland after moving from Northwest DC, when I was 12.

I don't even remember knowing or hearing my parents speaking of knowing anybody from Brandywine. But hell, people do move, so you never know, I reasoned.

After dinner, I got Quinton bathed and dressed for bed. We said our prayers and I kissed him good night. He was very intelligent for a five year old, reading like an 8 year old, and asking questions like a young philosopher. I loved him to death. I just never knew what to tell him whenever he'd ask about his dad.

At the thought of that man my blood would boil and my hatred or him would brew. Though I'd try not to reveal such emotions in front of Quinton, I knew he could tell because his inquires of his dad had started becoming few and far between.

That night I tossed and turned in my bed and for once it wasn't about that fateful night, but about this mystery person sending this money.

Who were they, and why did they feel compelled to help? Did they know my parents, did they know me? Did they know something about that night? Was it all a mistake?

Eventually these questions all banned together and collectively decided that sleep wasn't in the cards for me tonight.

I got up out of my bed and headed down to the kitchen where I poured myself a glass of milk. Then I went and had seat a on the porch. I looked around and noticed that every light in every house on the block was out. Not even the flickering lights of a television could be seen. North Carolina was different from Maryland and way different from DC. Right now there'd be men, women and even children out here chillin' on the block, laughing it up like it wasn't 2am. Cars would be bolting up and down the street with police sirens blaring in the distance. Gunshots would send folks in the house, but ten minutes later they'd be right back to chillin'.

Maryland was different also, some parts were anyway. Mostly kids hung out like that, but as the night wound down the numbers would drop. But at any given time of night you could at least see a bedroom light on, or the light from a TV going. Out here where my grandmother lived, they shut all the way down at about the same time. It was peaceful, but I missed the noise. I ended up falling asleep on the porch and was awakened by the paperboy.

"Morning Quinn." I heard him say as I was coming to.

"Morning Ralph, thanks." I said as I took the paper from him. I stood to stretch then I opened the screen door to go inside.

My grandmother was in the kitchen making breakfast like clockwork.

"Morning hun, how'd that old rocker treat ya last night?" She asked as I sat the paper on the counter.

"Saw me out there, huh?" I asked with a chuckle.

"I see everything. What were you doing out there anyway?" She asked.

"Couldn't sleep." I admitted.

"Had that dream again?" She asked now turning her attention towards me.

"Nah, just some things on my mind. But I'm okay though, I was able to think them through." I said to avoid a discussion.

"Yup, if there's anything that old rocker is good for, it's thinkin'." She said as she went back to cooking.

"Grandma, I've been thinking, I want to buy a car." I sort of blurted out.

"Heavens child, that came out like a waterfall." She said with a laugh.

"I know, soooo, what do you think?" I asked.

"I think that if this is what you want, I'll give Henry at the dealership a call and let him know we'll be there by 1 o'clock." She said.

"Great! Thanks grandma!" I said before I left the kitchen.

We went down to the dealership where I got a good deal on a dark blue 2007 Camry. I was in love.

A few days after the hype of owning a car had worn down, I found myself up in my room, looking at the papers my grandmother gave me about a week before.

73

I stared down at the address, as I normally did, but this time I wondered if I could find it. I got up and went over to my computer to pull up map quest. I put in the address and mapped it from our house in DC.

"Hmm, 37 miles, straight up Branch Avenue." I said reading the directions. I knew to get back to DC I'd have to take I-95 North and that it would be a long stretch, but definitely doable.

"Am I really thinkin about doin this?" I asked myself as I sat back in my chair.

I looked back over the directions on getting there, and it seemed simple enough. All I really needed to do was find a hotel not too far away, maybe somewhere in Waldorf.

"Oh my gawd, I am so doing this." I said aloud. I quickly printed the directions then I erased the browser information because I didn't want my grandmother to know what I was doing or where I was going.

I waited until nightfall after everyone was asleep to leave. I called and made hotel reservations for two days at a hotel in Waldorf. Afterwords I wrote my grandmother a note, before returning to my room to pack.

I went to my sons' room and watched him sleep for several minutes, then I kissed and hugged him before leaving out. I left the note for my grandmother on the kitchen table and went on my way.

I drove for about thirty minutes before I came to I-95N, then I followed it out on.

Driving through the night, listening to my cds, I was able to make it into Maryland in almost 4 hours.

It was now 7am and I was the epitome of drowsy. My mind and body got to a point where it no longer matter if I pulled over to rest, they were going to take what was theirs regardless. So I pulled into the parking lot of an IHOP and parked my car.

74

I stepped out and stretched the stiffness from my body before heading inside. I used the restroom, then I waited for them to seat me, I was hungry as hell.

My grandmother believes in eating dinner before the sun sets, and only healthy snacks there after.

After eating, I hung around for an extra hour then I paid for my food and left. With nowhere to go, and being extremely drowsy, I called the hotel to see if it were possible to check in early. I was elated when they said that I could. I got there in forty minutes, checked in, and went up to my room to collapse.

I woke up five hours later to the sound of my message notification. I looked down at my phone to see twenty missed calls and twenty voice mail messages all from my grandmother. I tossed the phone back onto the bed and headed for the shower.

After my shower I got dressed, grabbed my phone and the paper with the address on it and headed out.

It didn't take me too long to find the street that I was looking for, although I was surprised to see that it was a little strip mall. Anxious to get to the bottom of these letters I rushed down to the end of the strip mall where I presumed the address was, but to my dismay I discovered that the address wasn't even there.

"Wait, this can't be right." I said looking from the last building on the block back down to the paper with the address on it to make sure that I was looking for the right set of numbers.

I parked my car in front of the last store, which was a hardware store and got out to find out what was going on. I refused to believe that I had come this far to come up empty.

"This is crazy, how many streets can be named Hartville Rd in this small ass town anyway?" I asked myself before existing the car.

"Hey lil lady, what can I do you for?" Asked an older out of shaped man in a dingy white white beater.

"Sir, I'm looking for 6032, Hartville rd. You think you can help me?" I asked.

"I would if I could, but I can't so I won't. Just kiddin', well, I don't really know if that there address exists. This here is the last address on the block." The man said.

"Oh." I replied disappointed.

"Were you looking for a store? Maybe I can help ya find it." He said.

"No thanks, but thank you." I replied with a smile.

"Anytime gorgeous!" He called behind me as I walked out of the store. I got back into my car and tossed the paper into the passenger seat.

"I don't even believe this, I came all the way out here, for nothing." I said as I shook my head.

I started up my car and pulled out. As I drove along I noticed that the street lead into a wooded area where very large houses sat back far behind the trees.

"Hmm." I said as I noticed a few mailboxes. I drove closer and read the address on them as I passed.

"BINGO! 6032!" I exclaimed excited as hell. I looked up and saw a forest of trees down a long driveway leading to what looked like a mansion. I was a bit hesitant about going back there because after all, isn't that how scary movies started?

"Fuck it, I didn't come this far to punk out now." I said as I turned in to drive back to the house.

It was a five minute drive, but when I approached the house it looked like a whole other world. Big circle drive way, huge water fountain in the middle, large well groomed lawn, bushes shaped like animals. The place was huge. I parked my car at the entrance and got out.

Although I was scared to death, my curiosity pushed me forward. I walked up to the house and rang the doorbell, which played 'Reasons' by Earth Wind & Fire.

"Damn." I said with a laugh. A few seconds later the door opened but no one was standing there. I looked around for any sign of life, but there didn't seem to be any. However the house from what I could see of it was gorgeous. Huge spiral staircase, large works of art hanging covering the walls. It was amazing.

"Turn right, come back through the doors." I was startled by a voice I heard over an intercom system. But once I regained myself I followed suit.

When I got to where I was instructed to go, I saw a man sitting at an island in the middle of the kitchen drinking orange juice.

He was quite attractive, brown complexion, low haircut with a shape up, well-trimmed goatee, with a nice build.

"Hi." Was all that I could think to say. Although I longed for this moment, I wasn't quite verbally ready for it.

"What's up, what brings you here?" He asked before taking another sip.

"Uhm, I guess I'm looking for the owner. I have a couple personal questions that I wanted to ask." I said deeming him to be too young to be living this large. He couldn't have been no older than 30.

"I'm the owner, what's good?" He said as he stood to his feet to stretch.

"*You*?" I asked impressed.

"Yeah, me, what the fuck, a nigga can't live like this?" He asked taking up his orange juice and leaving the room.

"I never said that, I was just.. never mind." I said as I followed him into another room.

"So what are you, a detective or something?" He asked as I followed him into a room that looked like an arcade.

"Whoa." I said looking around at all the game systems and two 70" TV's that were mounted to the wall.

"So who are you again?" He asked as he sat on the lazy boy in front of the TV and grabbed a controller.

"My name is Quinn, I came because someone from this address has been sending these letters with checks, and I was curious as to why." I explained.

He stopped playing the game and looked over at me for a few seconds as though he were trying to figure something out. Then his facial expression changed to a half smile.

"Let me see that real quick." He said reaching for the letters. He looked them over, then he handed them back to me.

"Hmm." Was his only response.

"Well, are they from you?" I asked watching him getting back into his game.

"yeah, they from me." He replied never taking his eyes off the screen.

"But why, why are you helping us?" I asked as I sat on the lazy boy next to his.

"What, you don't need it?" He asked still into his game.

"I mean, it helps, but I just want to know why. What's it to you to help us?" I asked. He turned to look at me.

"Hold up, you drove all the way here from North Carolina, just to ask me this?" He asked confused.

"I did." I replied feeling a little silly.

"What's it to you, to want to know why, that bad?" He asked.

I sat back in the lazy boy and shook my head.

"Because I don't just want to know why, I need to know why." I said looking over at him.

"Where you staying?" He asked after a few seconds of silence.

"The holiday inn in Waldorf." I replied.

"Stay here with me. I'll take care of the hotel." He said.

"I don't even *know* you." I said as if the idea was absurd.

"Yet you drove almost 300 miles to meet me." He said.

"True." I replied shaking my head at myself.

"I'll set you up in one of the guest rooms." He said as he stood to his feet.

"You're still helping me, but you won't tell me why, or even who you are." I said.

"All will be revealed in due time. By the way, my name is Q" he said.

"That's not a name." I said.

"It's not your name, but it is mine. Second floor, third room. That's where you'll be staying." He said before leaving the room.

I stood up and wandered the house until I came across an elevator.

"What in the world?" I asked. I shook my head and pushed the up button. When the doors opened I stepped inside.

"What floor sexy?" I heard a woman's computerized voice ask

"Uh, second." I replied.

"Sorry, don't recognize voice, press the number on the panel." The voice said. I chuckled and pressed the number two.

"Second floor." The computerized voice said as the doors opened. I stepped off and looked around. The upstairs was as extravagant as the downstairs.

I turned right and counted out the rooms which were far apart. When I got to the third room I opened the door to find a huge suite.

The room was bigger than the first floor at my grandmother's home. Three huge Windows reaching from floor to ceiling. King size bed, a breakfast nook, a balcony, 52 inch television mounted to the wall, a bar, and a music system.

Never had I been in a place so extravagant. I walked over and sat on the bed as I tried to take it all in. A few moments later I heard a knock at my door and looked over to see Q standing there.

"Hey." I said as I stood up.

"Hey, so you feeling the room?" He asked as he stepped inside.

"Like you wouldn't believe." I replied.

"Yeah, I love this house." He said more to himself.

"So what are you, some kinda drug lord?" I asked really believing that he'd tell me.

He broke out into laughter.

"Nah baby girl, that's not me, I mean once upon a time, but not in many years." He finally said after containing his laughter.

"Then how?" I asked.

"Everything I have, I worked for." He said with a shrug.

"So it's all legit?" I asked.

"Legit by whose standards?" He asked.

"The *law*!" I replied in my 'duh' voice.

"Then yeah." He stated matter of factly.

"That didn't sound too convincing." I said raising an eyebrow.

"As corrupt as the law is, my shit is A-100. Come on, I wanna show you something." He said before turning to leave.

I slowly followed him as I tried to process what he'd just said. We walked through the house and out the back.

"But if you say the..." I started still trying to piece together what he was saying.

"Shhh, what you know about this?" He asked interrupting me as he stretched his arms out wide. I looked up and saw the most beautiful well-kept lake stretching the length of his backyard.

"This is beautiful!" I said as I walked out in front of him.

"You wanna go in?" He asked.

"What's this, a movie about farm life? I'm not swimming in no lake." I retorted

"No, I mean have a boat." He said.

"Oh, okay." I replied a little embarrassed.

"Follow me." He said with a chuckle.

We walked out to the docks where he proceeded to unlock a boat. I'm thinking he had a regular sailboat, this fool had what looked like a mini yacht.

"Do you do everything big?" I asked as he helped me aboard.

"Of course, or why do it at all?" He said.

He walked over and started up the boat, slowly we began to move.

"So where are you from, Q?" I asked.

"Here." He replied casually.

"Born and raised?" I asked.

"Born in South East, raised in Northwest." He said.

"So you're from the city." I said referring to DC.

"All day, Maryland girl." He said teasingly

"Maryland is cool, but I'm originally from uptown." I said.

"Well you in North Carolina now." He said as he turned the sail.

"Yeah." I replied dully, not wishing to reveal why, but it did bring me back to my original question.

"So, you never did tell me why you've been sending us money." I said.

"Nope, I sure didn't." He replied taking a seat.

"Are you going to?" I asked.

He looked up at me for a few seconds before Answering.

"I will, just chill with me for a lil bit, okay." He said.

"Did you know my parents, did you know me?" I asked.

"This is not chillin'." He replied sounding a little annoyed as he stood to his feet to walk over to the railing.

"I came a long way for some answers, and I want them." I demanded.

"And you'll get them, but on *my* time." He said turning back around to face me.

I looked at him for a few seconds matching his stare before breaking it. Then sighed and turned my attention to the water and the beautiful landscape.

"Come look at this." He called over to me after several moments of silence.

I stood up and walked over to see what seemed to fascinate him so. It was the sun setting over the treetops. It was gorgeous.

"You get to see this every day?" I said as I looked on.

"Yeah, amazing right?" He asked.

"Absolutely." I said.

"You hungry?" He asked turning his attention towards me.

"yeah, I haven't eaten since breakfast." I replied touching my stomach.

"yeah, I just heard it growl at me. Come on, we're gonna head back." He said as he steered the boat back to the dock.

Back in the house I found my clothing in my bedroom already waiting for me. I showered and dressed then he took us to a very romantic outdoor candle lit restaurant. There was a live band playing old school melodies. The tables were set up on a raised platform that over looked a river. There were dim lamp post placed along the outside of the platform giving the little restaurant its light.

"This atmosphere is so perfect." I said gazing about.

"Yeah, it is." He replied.

"So then why would you bring me here?" I asked blushing.

He shook his head and shrugged his shoulders.

"Why not?" He asked.

"Because I'm no one special, I mean, not to you anyway." I said.

"You don't know that." He replied.

"So you *do* know me?" I asked.

"Dance with me." He said as he held his hand out for me to take. I took it and stood up with him. He walked me out to the dance floor and led me into a slow dance.

I felt him slide his arms around me and he held me in his arms. It felt good, I had never been held by a man, I was always too afraid to get close. He gently pushed me out and spinned me around, then he brought me back but this time, not as close. We danced all of my worries and cares away and I found my mind at peace for the first time in a long time.

After we ate we took a stroll along the water front. Everything was so perfect I never wanted this night to end.

We were quiet during most of the walk. Lost in our own little worlds as I watched the water and he seemed to be watching the sky.

"Q, can I ask you a question?" I asked breaking the silence.

"What's up?" He asked as he stopped walking.

"Why are you doing all of this?" I asked.

"What's all this?" He asked

"Letting me stay at your place, the boat ride, the dinner, this walk, the money. What's it all for?" I asked.

He looked away and shook his head as though he didn't have an answer.

"I'm not sure really. I guess I just wanted to show you something." He said.

"What's that?" I asked

"*Me.*" He said

"You're not making sense Q." I said.

"I know, but it will make sense, come on, let's go." He said.

We walked back up to the parking lot where the limo was waiting. We got in and rode back to his place in silence. Once there he walked me to the elevator.

"Q, thank you for everything." I said as I gave him a slight hug. He looked at me like he wanted to kiss me. It made me nervous because I have never been kissed.

"I knew you were coming." He said.

"How?" I asked just above a whisper.

"I could feel it." He replied

"So you're finally admitting that you do know me?" I asked.

"Yes." He replied.

"How?" I asked.

"It'll come to you, go to sleep." He said as he reached behind me to push to button to open the elevator doors. Then he turned to leave.

Later that night I lay in bed and relived the moments of the day. This was the most romantic day of my life. I felt things I never knew I could feel. And he was the perfect gentlemen the whole time.

I fell asleep with these thoughts running through my head. But while my dreams started off sweet, my mind drifted back to that night six years earlier, and again I woke up in a cold sweat. But this time, I felt very odd. I had an eerie feeling like the dream wasn't over.

I got up and stumbled out of my room and made my way to the stairs. My mind kept flashing visions of the night my parents were killed and I couldn't shake them. I found my way to the kitchen and went into the refrigerator to get myself some Orange juice. I wasn't thirsty per se, I just need to try to refocus my mind on something else.

After I filled a cup I kept trying to shake my dream as well as attempt to figure out why it still felt so alive in me. I was awake now, the feeling should have faded and my mind should be at ease, but it just wouldn't relax.

As I was trying to figure out what was happening, I heard footsteps leading to the kitchen, and they triggered something in my mind as it began to race over my dream faster and faster but this time incorporating the events of yesterday until I made the connection.

"Oh my God" I said as the glass slipped from my hand.

"Whoa, you okay?" Q asked as he entered the kitchen.

"It was *you*!" I said looking at him as an anger I never before experienced slowly consumed me. Q was the killer, he was the man who killed my parents and raped me. He's the father of my son.

"Yes, it's me." He said calmly.

"I fuckin hate you, you took my whole life away!" I screamed.

"I know." He replied still calmly.

"You knew it was me this whole time? You did all that stuff, did you think it was going to make up for it?!" I asked as I felt myself going crazy with rage.

"Nothing I can say or do will change what I did, or what I took from you." He said as he eased his way over to me.

"You took my life, you took my life!" I screamed over and over again as I started crying hysterically. My body began to shake and tremble. He tried put his arms around me but I punched him in the face and kept swinging. He held me tighter as I struggled against him. I struggled with everything I had, until I couldn't fight anymore.

He lift me up into his arms and carried me to the bedroom where he lay me on the bed and covered me with a blanket.

"You took my life." I said looking at him as new tears began to fall.

He nodded his head as a tear escaped his eye.

"I know." He said before he walked away. I was so overwhelmed with so many emotions that I felt as though I was starting to drown in them. Eventually I rocked myself to sleep.

I woke up hours later feeling only a little better. I got out of bed and went back downstairs where I found Q sitting in the living room on the couch. He had a glass of cognac in his had that he had been sipping on while gazing out of the picture window.

"I need to know why." I said as I sat on the loveseat across from him. He took another sip before sitting forward on the couch.

"You're better off with what you think you know." He said before sitting the glass on the coffee table.

"I have a right to know what happened." I demanded.

"You do, but I'd rather you keep the same good thoughts you have about your daddy, and leave me as the monster." He said

"You will always be a monster to me. I just want to know why." I said snapped.

"Fine, your daddy was a drug Lord. A very powerful one. I was one of his top assassins. He never hired me directly, so he never met me personally. Whenever the money makers needed shit done, they knew to hit me up. My indirect comradery with him was good until he set my little sister up." He explained.

"Wait, hold up, so I'm supposed to believe my dad was big time in the drug game?" I asked in sheer disbelief.

"He was the man" Q said replied plain and simple.

"Then why we ain't live it?" I asked as I folded my arms

"For the same reason he never got busted, he was smart, until he crossed me." Q said

"And how'd he do that?" I asked.

"As I was saying, he set my sister up. He wanted her to be his mistress, she declined, so he used some strag bitches to trick her into snorting coke. She got hooked and he used her. When he was done, he killed her. My sister was 17 when she died." Q explained.

"I'm sorry about your sister, but how can you be so sure it was my dad's doing?" I asked.

"The grapevine ain't just a song. And you'd be surprised how quickly a nigga will go from gangsta to informant when he got a shotgun in his face." Q said explained.

"So what you did to *us*, was to get back at my *dad*." I said.

He nodded his head.

"He slutted my sister out, he had her fuckin and suckin' everybody, even animals, and he videoed that shit." Q said as he crushed his glass in his hands.

"Q, I'm sorry." I said shaking my head.

"Don't be, because I'm not sorry." He said.

"Not even for what you did to me?" I asked looking down at my fingers.

"I'm sorry that I had to take your innocence." He admitted.

"I have nightmares about that night all the time." I said.

"Me too, but the only thing in my dreams are you." He said.

I looked up at him shocked.

"You know, we have a son." I said.

He nodded his head yes.

"I named him Quinton. He has your eyes." I said softy.

"I hope not." He said.

"What?" I asked confused.

"All I've seen is fear and death. I don't want that for him. I kill better than I can do anything else. That's all I have to pass on, this curse I built my life off of." He said.

"So you'll never meet him?" I asked.

"I'm a monster Quinn, its bad enough he has my blood in his veins." Q said.

"You don't have to be anything that you don't want to be." I said as I walked over and sat next to him.

He looked at me with a slight smile.

"I see I didn't take all of your innocence." He said as he moved my hair away from my face.

"Last night, while we were dancing, and you spinned me around. Why didn't you hold me close the way you did before?" I asked as the memory entered my thoughts.

"Because I felt your heart beat." He said.

"I don't understand." I said

"Has a man ever held you in his arms, kissed or touched you?" He asked.

"No." I replied bashfully.

"I can't really explain it Quinn, your signals said stop." He said.

"But it felt good." I said

"It's made to feel good, but that don't mean you're ready for it." He said.

"So now what?" I asked with a shrug, not liking the feeling of vulnerability that was starting to come for me.

89

"Now, you go back home better informed, and I go back to my life of solitude." He said with a sigh.

"That's it, just like that?" I asked.

"Quinn, nothing has changed. I'm still the man who took your life away. The monster that haunts your dreams. I'm a natural born killer. It's who I am. It's a burden I wear like a weight vest every day of my life." He said.

"But you can change." I said.

"I'll never change, this is me. It's been me for over half my life and will be me for the remainder." He said. I looked at him but said nothing, there was nothing more to say. It was obvious that his couldn't be changed.

After lunch I went up to my room to pack my things. I had planned to drive back home that day.

I hadn't spoken to my grandmother since I left, so I knew she was worried sick, even though I left her a note. And poor Quinton was probably so upset, we haven't been apart this long since his birth.

I regretted leaving them clueless, but it was something I felt I had to do. Now that I did it, I felt different, less confused and more complete.

"Hey." I heard Q's voice say as he knocked on the door.

"Hey." I replied as I zipped my bag.

"I didn't want you to take that drive, at least not alone. So I went on ahead and got you a plane ticket." He said handing me a first class ticket.

"But my car." I said.

"It'll be waiting for you at the valet at the airport in North Carolina" He said.

"You always put plans in motion before I can protest." I said shaking my head.

"Do you have a protest against me trying to make your life easier?" He asked.

"How long do you plan on being my guardian angel, Q?" I asked as I stood up and put my bag on my shoulder.

"Forever." He replied.

"Why?" I asked back.

"I don't know, maybe because I took your life, maybe because you have my son, or maybe because you're the only one I have ever had remorse for, behind what I did." He said with a shrug.

"To my family?" I asked.

"No, to you." He said.

I walked over and put my arms around his neck. He hesitated for a few seconds before sliding his arms around my waist.

"I can feel your heartbeat." He whispered to me.

"Good." I replied looking into his eyes. I moved forward to kiss his lips, but he put his head down.

"No, your first kiss will not be with a monster." He said.

"But I want to." I said ignoring what he said.

"You're just emotional right now, and I'd be an even dirtier nigga than I already am if I played into that." He said as he let me go.

"You think too much." I said.

"Yeah, so do you, and I don't want you goin back home feelin' even more fucked up that you allowed yourself to get close enough to your parents killer, to let him be your first kiss. How twisted is that? How fucked up would you be when you woke up in the morning?" He asked.

"It sounds like you want me to hate you." I said.

"Quinn, I just want you to be realistic. Last night, I was the star of your nightmare. Today you want to kiss me?" He said.

I shook my head.

"okay, I get it." I said as I walked towards the door.

"You don't, but you will." He said.

I turned around to look at him, then I left the room.

When I got downstairs I heard a horn blowing outside.

"That's your car to take you to the airport." He said as he walked over to open the door.

"Well, I guess this is goodbye." I said.

"I'm glad you came." He said.

"Thank you for the closure." I said.

He nodded his head.

We hugged and then I turned to head outside. There was a man in a chauffeur's hat standing at the back door of a Lincoln. I walked down the steps to meet him.

"Quinn, I need you to promise me something." He called behind me.

"What?" I asked as I turned around to face him.

"That, no matter what you see on your way out of here, you'll keep going. Don't come back." He said.

"Huh?" I asked confused.

"Just promise me you'll keep going." He said.

"Okay, I promise." I said.

He nodded his head. I turned to head towards the car, then I turned my attention back towards him.

"Quinton." He said.

"What?" I asked wondering how he knew what I was going to ask him.

"My name, Q stands for Quinton." He said.

My heart smiled and so did I. Quinton smiled too.

I got into the car and the door was closed behind me. I looked up at Q who was watching me as the driver started driving away.

As soon as we got out of the driveway I saw a fleet of police cars rush by and turn in, and a helicopter flying overhead.

"Q." I said as I turned to see them all heading for his house.

One month later I received a letter in the mail with no return address. It was from Quinton, it read.

Dear Quinn,

I'm sorry that I'm just writing you, I know that you must've been filled with questions when you saw the police coming to my home. I had been struggling with myself for a long time over what I did to you. While I feel no regret for killing the man who killed my sister, I regret what I did to you. I don't know why, just another one of life's mysteries, I guess. When I told you I felt you coming it's because I did. Maybe that night when we connected, I took a piece of your spirit with me, and maybe it's because of that, I was able to feel everything you felt. I don't know, I'm just trying to understand all of this. Anyway, I turned myself in, that's why you saw all the police coming for me. I'm doing life, no parole. But not like regular people, because they know that much of my money can be tied to many political and judicial figures. So to save their own asses, their letting me live how I please. I won't tell you where I am, but I'm good, and I just want you to know that I will be your guardian angel for the rest of my life. Take care of my son, tell him whatever you want about me, but also tell him that I love him, and above all else, I want him to be a better man than me. Take care beautiful, live happy, live free.

-Quinton

I read the letter 3 times before folding it up and stuffing it into my box before placing it into the moving truck with the rest of me and Quinton's things. After my journey I was able to gain inner peace.

The nightmares stopped, and I was no longer afraid. I felt stronger and more secure, and able to stand on my own two feet. I got a good job thanks to my grandmother's connections and a place of my own. Q kept his word and saw to it that we never wanted for anything, but above all that, he gave me something more valuable than money, he gave me closure, and it changed my whole life, for the better.

THE END

Questions / Comments / Concerns ? Connect with the Author via:

- **Facebook: Nikida Bellezza**
- **IG: Nikida_Bellezza**
- **Twitter: @NikidaBellezza**

Want More Titles By Nikida Bellezza?

Visit Amazon.com and Type Nikida Bellezza into the search to find the following titles

- **Goodbye (a short)**
- **Rain of Emotions: Drops of Poetry (Poetry)**
- **Sidechick Blues**
- **Sidechick Blues The Filler**
- **Sidechick Blues The Plot-- The Plot is a combination of Sidechick Blues & Sidechick Blues Filler along with a little background info on the characters.**

Thank You For Reading!!

/

www.ingramcontent.com/pod-product-compliance
Lightning Source LLC
Chambersburg PA
CBHW070804120626
46557CB00002B/714